HOUSE BENEATH THE BRIDGE

IAIN ROB WRIGHT

WANT FREE BOOKS?

Don't miss out on your FREE Iain Rob Wright horror starter pack. Five free bestselling horror novels sent straight to your inbox. No strings attached.

For more information just visit this page:
www.iainrobwright.com/free-starter-pack/

In addition, you can also save money by purchasing books in extra-value box sets. Grab yours now.

Boxset 1
Sam, ASBO, The Final Winter, The Housemates, Sea Sick

Boxset 2
Ravage, Savage, Animal Kingdom, The Picture Frame, 2389, The Peeling Omnibus, Slasher, Soft Target, A-Z of Horror Vol 1

To feed my children with the words I write...
A dream.

I don't like to commit myself about heaven and hell - you see, I have friends in both places.

— **Mark Twain**

The plain truth is that the period I study is the 16th century, and they were absolutely obsessed with witches and spiritual beings.

—**J. B. Priestley**

You'll simply never understand the true nature of sacrifice.

—**May Morrison, The Wicker Man; British Lion, 1973**

CHAPTER 1

Father Cotton clutched the bible against his chest and spat fury beneath his fluttering cowl. A wind picked up and carried a fine mist across the river, but it would not affect his focus. "The Lord sees your sin, creature, and denies you entry to paradise. What have you say? Speak now, or forever hold your peace."

"I am innocent, I swear it," cried the fiend, Emily Tanner, fighting the Hessian ropes binding her to the oak's broad trunk. The ancient tree had been healthy and strong just one week ago, but now it withered and listed precariously over the river. "I have done nothing! Where is my husband? Jonathan, where are you, my love?"

The village tailor emerged from the crowd, bleary-eyed and holding Martha Hamleigh in his arms. The grieving mother sobbed and made a sound akin to a wounded lamb. Her long brown hair mingled with Jonathan's and created an unruly nest. "I am here, Emily," he said. "As much as I wish it were not so."

Emily's face lit up at the sight of her spouse, but Father Cotton saw it for what it was—a perverse replica of human emotion—and it sickened him. Her voice was thick with mock-innocence as she spoke. "My love, help me!" she begged. Her golden hair framed her face in a picture of naïve innocence. "Tell them I am not what they say. I would never hurt a child. Nev-"

"Enough, Emily!" Jonathan was rubbing Martha's back, but her sobs continued to rise. "You are my wife, and I love you—God forgive me for how much I love you, but I cannot deny what I have seen. You returned to our home at an ungodly hour—a lost siren, naked and muddied by the river. There is too much evidence of your crimes to deny. Our vows lay broken, and my obligation to you with them. Martha is the victim here, Emily. You took her children both. Dear Lord, you butchered them." He covered his mouth for to prevent expelling his supper. Who could blame the poor man for his disgust?

Emily fought against her bonds again. "Martha lies! I am innocent. Does ten years of marriage mean nothing, dear husband?"

Father Cotton had heard enough and thrust out his bible like a shield, its pages fluttering in the wind. "You have chance to repent, creature, but seek instead to bend and manipulate. To ask Jonathan to intervene now is to condemn his soul alongside your own. You were witnessed at the crime scene, Emily Tanner, young blood still staining your hands. The Church finds you guilty of witchcraft!"

"You mean *YOU* find me guilty of witchcraft, Father Cotton. Damn you and your blind righteousness!" She glowered upon every man, woman, and child assembled by the riverside, and directed her judgement at them all. "Damn you all to the darkest hell. I am no witch. I am no child butcher. It is all of you who are guilty. YOU who judge with fear and loathing, while forsaking love and compassion. For years I have lived amongst you. Your neighbour, your friend..." she looked at Jonathan. "Your wife!"

"And you have given your husband no family," someone shouted. "The ungodly cannot bare children. They are cursed barren. Harlot!"

"Witch!"

"Whore!"

"Siren!"

Emily spotted one of her hecklers—Thompson, the widowed sheep farmer—and whipped a gaze upon him so fierce that he shrank back into the crowd like a bleating calf. Even Father Cotton shuddered at the sheer malice in the creature's eyes. To think he had judged her a simple woman for so many years. In this, he had truly failed.

"It is you who will be cursed if you do this!" Emily promised the crowd, her venom only increasing. "Your souls will burn in the Abyss. You shall feed on mud and rotting flesh like meal worms."

Thompson, the widow, re-emerged and thrust a trembling finger at her. "She admits it! She places a hex upon us! A witch!"

"Lies!" shouted Emily. "All lies. Where is the abbot? Does he know you intend murder this night, Father? Has the Church not tired of your unceasing condemnations? Is it not your nature that should stand judged?"

Father Cotton gritted his teeth and tried not to lose composure. This was the way of darkness—to seek out the light and try to extinguish it. This witch would not pollute his belief in himself. He would not allow it. "The abbot is infirmed due to a hex most likely placed upon his soul by you!" A howling gust rose up and buffeted his woollen habit, aggravating the tender wounds beneath. "We found his Holiness lying in his vestry, furnace-hot and babbling."

"A simple fever, surely?" cried Emily.

"Quiet beast! Your corruption is at an end. Tonight the village shall weep for the woman you were, and celebrate the vanquishing of the evil you have become. May your butchered victims rest in a peace you shall never know."

Emily thrashed against her bonds like a wild animal, drawing blood from her slender wrists. She kicked her bare feet amongst the leaves and flicked them at the crowd—a defiant, yet ineffectual gesture. "I wish upon you eternal agony," she screeched, tears soaking her face. "I will see it so!"

Father Cotton gave no reply. He returned the bible to his chest and placed out an open hand, summoning Jonathan, who passed him a lit torch. Emily moaned at her husband's betrayal, and he sheepishly rejoined the crowd. Father Cotton pitied the heartbroken tailor, for it was the truest of tortures for a righteous man to face—the condemnation of a loved one. The spurning of a wife was perhaps the pinnacle of righteous sacrifice. His reward would come in the next life.

Father Cotton strode towards the pyre, torch lofted above his head. "Emily Tanner. As your flesh burns and agony cleanses you, Heaven will not await. Consider your misdeeds, but know that no chance for atonement shall come. Eternity is a barren wasteland of everlasting solitude to you."

"I did not kill the Hamleigh twins! You condemn an innocent woman this night, and you shall know the consequences."

Father Cotton dropped the torch into the crisp, dead leaves. The conflagration was immediate. Flames leapt in a circle around Emily's feet and she screamed, but only in fear just now, for the pain was yet to begin. The dusk turned orange, and the crowd looked upon one another's faces. None showed regret. They did the Lord's work today: ending the life of a child killer.

Emily's screams halted as she bit down on her tongue. More tears came, along with blood from her mouth. The look she gave the crowd was no longer condemning, but pleading. All evil quivered before the glory of God, and Father Cotton was a beacon shining said glory unto every patch of shadow. He would hold the divine image of Emily's broken will in his mind tonight as he flagellated himself before the statue of Saint Adolphus, the Martyr. No better way to wash the wretchedness from his soul.

Tomorrow, there would more glory to shine.

Emily's screams increased pitch. Flames circled inward, devouring the dry leaves piled at her feet. Her pale skin turned pink, and blistered, while the stench of burning meat made those in the crowd cover their noses. These were godly people, and watching human flesh burn was a dark deed. Yet it was necessary. All must see justice done this night. The village needed to shed its sin alongside Emily Tanner.

Forgive us Lord for our sins.

Emily's woollen nightdress ignited, and her high-pitched screams turned low and bovine. In unison, and without prompting, the villagers began chanting the Lord's prayer.

"Our Father, which art in heaven, hallowed be thy name. Thy kingdom come, thy will be done in earth as it is in Heaven. Give us this day our daily bread, and forgive us our trespasses, as we forgive them that trespass against us. And lead us not into temptation, but deliver us from evil."

The sinew of Emily's legs reduced to fat, spitting from her bones as her body melted. Blood turned black and curdled. Her nightdress shrivelled away to nothing and exposed her nakedness.

The points of her breasts popped like carbuncles and drizzled down her chest. Silky golden hair curled in on itself and smoked before falling away from her glistening scalp. Then her eyes rolled back in her head and her bellows became whimpers. A prayer-length later Emily Tanner was a charred skull staring back at them.

Then the flames leapt higher into the night sky and she vanished from them forever.

But the blackened oak tree remained. Even in the inferno, it persisted holding onto the blackened earth. Father Cotton would command the monks from the abbey to fell the ungodly thing at dawn, but first he turned to the crowd. "We did the Lord's work today, my children. Be not troubled, for the righteous act is never the easy one. Go home to your loved ones and pray, for tomorrow is another day."

A roaring gust came off the river, summoned by the hungry fire. Hot air drew sweat from the brows of those closest, including Father Cotton, and many moved away. Father Cotton clutched his bible in one hand and used his other to wrangle the hair from his face. As he did so, pain flared in his left eyelid. "Jesus Mary!"

"Father?" said Jonathan, splitting from the crowd and hurrying to his aid. "What is wrong?"

Father Cotton pressed his palm against his burning eyelid and tried to push the pain away. "It is nothing, good Jonathan. An ember from the flames. We should depart this place, lest its echoes haunt us too long."

"Of course, Father."

Jonathan attempted to ease him away, but he shrugged the gesture off, angered by the pain still flaring in his eyelid and baleful of pity from a lowly man such as Jonathan. "I hope days to come do not reveal you complicit in your wife's actions, Jonathan Tanner. May the Lord strike you to ash if you are."

Jonathan staggered as if struck. "I swear it, Father. I had no idea. If I had known..."

An angry buzz drowned out Jonathan's words and indeed replaced all sound in the space beside the river. The departing crowd stopped and glanced back at the pyre. The inferno had risen high, illuminating the sky red, but its spreading glow was not yet finished. Orange tendrils dispelled the dusk in every direction. Embers spewed forth into the frigid gloom like a swarm of bees.

A literal swarm.

Fiery specks fluttered on the air, almost serenely, but then they descended savagely upon the crowd. The villagers cried out in pain and confusion. Father Cotton turned a full circle, trying to decipher the Lord's will in what he was seeing.

What *was* he seeing?

His eyes confused, now buzzing filled his ears.

Nearby, Jonathan batted at himself hysterically, an angry welt rising quickly on one cheek. A wasp formed of flame and crawled along his jawline. "It's Emily," he cried. "She has cast a hex upon us. She swore it. Dear God, what folly have we brought?"

Father Cotton watched the pyre in awe, its flames whipping like enlivened sprites. Thousands more spiteful embers grabbed hold of the wind and descended upon the screaming villagers, wrenching out their torment, but a separate swarm now headed toward him alone, marking him out, and chattering in his ears so loud his brain ached. He threw up his arms to shield himself, dropping his bible in the slick, black mud. His mouth opened to scream, but before he could make a sound, searing agony filled his throat. Jonathan, prisoner to his own panic, collided with him and knocked them both to the ground. From on his back, Father Cotton stared into the flames. The shadow of a woman looked back at him. Then, a hundred embers engulfed his face and stung the sight from his eyes.

Unable to see, unable to speak, he prayed to the Lord for help.

But the Lord was not there.

CHAPTER 2

"So, you'll call me when you get to your sister's?" said Tom as he exited the highway and joined a roundabout decorated with dainty pink flowers.

Sophie pressed her forehead against the window and stared out at the drizzle. Apt weather for how she was feeling. "What's the point?" she said. "We're getting divorced, Tom. We don't need to check in with each other anymore."

Tom squeezed the steering wheel—she could tell because his knuckles whitened and his wedding ring lifted away from his finger. "Just because you don't want to be my wife anymore doesn't mean you're dead to me, Soph! Let me know you're safe so I can sleep tonight, yes?"

"I'm not your concern anymore."

"I'll decide when you're no longer my concern."

Sophie pulled her head away from the window, leaving makeup on the glass, and looked at him. She was too tired to argue—the kind of tired that came from being so so unhappy for so so long. "Fine. I'll call you once I get there, but that's it. We need space so we can accept things. Staying in contact will only make it harder."

Tom fell silent, breathing audibly through his nose. Eyes still on the road, he nodded a fraction. "I know."

Sophie returned her forehead to the window.

They came off the roundabout and Tom took the exit marked

'Cottontree'. It was the village of her birth, and she was loath returning to it, but she had no place else to go. Her loopy sister was the only family she had left, and the sad old cow had never left the home they grew up in. Even now, Sophie could see the place hadn't changed at all—the same dreary, depressing place it had always been. They passed by the school she attended as a child and she closed her eyes in misery.

"It's nice," said Tom, staring at St Thomas's chapel on the corner of the single main road. "Can't believe I haven't been here before, all the years we've been married."

"I hate it here. Can't believe I'm back."

He sighed. "I said you didn't have to move out. We could've made something work."

Sophie moaned. Tom was awful at standing by his decisions, always so full of self-doubt. "Tom, I can't stand to look at you."

"Wow, thanks! What the hell did I do?"

She sighed and pulled her head away from the window again. "No, I don't mean it like that. I mean, I can't take being guilty anymore. The way you make me feel... No more, okay? Let's just get this over with."

He fell silent again, glaring through the windscreen at the drizzle-soaked road. Eventually he muttered something, "I'm sorry, Soph."

She went back to looking out the window. "Me too."

Tom slowed down past the church, shifting his Mercedes into 2nd. "Where do I go from here?"

She pointed ahead, remembering the village like she'd left it yesterday instead of twenty years ago. "Take the next left over the bridge. It'll take you across the river. My mom's house is right after."

"You still call it your mom's house?"

"I suppose so. The past is hard to forget."

Tom nodded and took the turning towards the bridge. "It certainly is."

☙☙

GWEN'S HANDS TREMBLED AS THEY GRIPPED THE FUZZY PINK

steering wheel. Passing her test first time meant she knew how to drive, right? So why did it terrify her being out like this without an instructor? Having fought so long to be an adult, now she doubted she could be one. In fact, she wanted to jump beneath her duvet and surround herself with teddy bears.

"Hell yes, bitches!" Stacey hadn't shut up for the last two miles —or since she'd first learned to talk really—but she was now more excitable than ever. "This is so fucking cool, Gwen. We can go anywhere. Fuck Cottontree, and fuck the losers who live here." She clutched the thick, white-gold necklace with her name emblazoned on it and pressed it up against the passenger window. "Stacey Chatwin is out of here, bitches!"

"We can go somewhere with a cinema," Mia chirped from the back seat. As usual, she played nervously with her waist-length brown hair. Gwen loved her, but she needed to let her mom get her to a salon before they named her the Pakistani Rapunzel.

Time to grow up for all of us, she thought. *Not just me.*

"Let's start with a few laps around the block, guys. This is my first time out on my own."

"You're not on your own," said Stacey. "You're with us. And screw sticking to the village. Take the bridge, and let's get the fuck out of here. Let's go down the rugby club in town."

"It's up to Gwen," said Mia. "It's her car."

Stacey whirled in the front seat to glare at her. "Don't be such a pussy, Mia. You don't want to stay in Cottontree any more than I do. We can find some real men at the rugby club. Maybe one of them will take those reigns of yours and give you a nice hard ride before you get married off."

Mia tutted in frustration. "I've told you before, my parents don't want an arranged marriage for me."

"That's just what they say now because they can't find anyone to take you on. Maybe Gwen's brother will volunteer. He talked to you that one time, remember? I think you were blocking his way to the fridge."

Stacey said it in jest, but Gwen glanced in the rearview mirror and saw Mia blush and look away humiliated. Stacey's coarse mouth often got the better of their meeker friend. Such a bitch.

"Fine. I'll take us out of town," said Gwen. "Just keep quiet until I get my wits about me, okay, Stacey? You haven't even taken your first driving lesson yet, so you have no idea how scary this is, so stop being such a brat!"

Stacey put a hand on Gwen's thigh and squeezed. "Relax girl, you're doing great."

"I don't want to crash."

"You won't! I guaran-fucking-tee it."

"Come on, Brandon! Job's a good'un so let's get on to the next." His dad climbed into the truck before Brandon had even removed his work gloves. He was having trouble keeping pace with his old man. It was like he needed to be glued to him every second or get left behind.

"Just let me get my tools, dad."

"Hurry up, lad. We get this next job done, we can have a pint down the Archers before we knock off for the day. Work hard, play hard, that's the name of the game. It'll keep you out of that bloody hovel you call a bedroom, and get you mixing with normal blokes."

Brandon gathered the shovels but struggled to hold them all at once. He waddled along the path with them like an arthritic porcupine before awkwardly hoisting everything up into the truck's rear bed. The largest of the shovels hit the rear panel and bounced off onto the road. "Bugger it!"

"Come on, Bran! Stop pissing about."

"Sorry, dad!" He picked up the shovel and lobbed it in with the others. He was about to grab a strap and fasten everything down, but his dad sounded the horn and made him jump. "Okay, okay, I'm coming!"

By the time he leapt into the passenger seat, his dad had shifted into first and took off. "You really want that pint, huh, dad?"

"What you trying to say, lad? I'd just rather get this next job done in an hour and go the pub, than spend two hours on it and go home to your ma's cooking. You need to mix more."

Brandon rolled his eyes. "So, what is the next job?"

"Same as the one we just finished. Got to build a mound to stop the Gypos camping on the playing fields."

"Aren't they Travellers, not 'Gypos'?"

His dad threw the truck around a corner and shrugged. "What's the difference?"

"I... don't know."

"Well, the village council has had enough of 'em messing the place up, so we get paid to shovel piles of mud at the roadside to keep their caravans off. Bryne's meeting us there with the digger. He was expecting us twenty minutes ago."

"Great!" Brandon hated his uncle Bryne. The guy was a pisshead and stunk of B.O. His favourite hobby was taking the micky out of everyone, and especially enjoyed it when Brandon was the target. A right wanker. Brandon thought about slashing his tyres sometimes, or slipping bleach in his pint and watching him clutch his throat in agony. Now *that* would be funny.

They sped towards Old Abbey Bridge and passed the playing fields next to the supermarket. Two cars were coming in the opposite direction, but his dad didn't decelerate for them—he who drives the white van has the right of way, he always said—and as the truck reached the bridge's narrow peak, a thud sounded from the rear bed.

Brandon's dad glared at him, his thick black eyebrows threatening to leap out and smother him. "You strap down the tools, lad?"

"No, you didn't give me ti—" There was another thud. His dad swore and stamped on the brake. It wasn't the smartest thing to do.

Brandon's jaw dropped as he watched two shovels and a rake fly out from behind the truck and launch across the bridge just as the other two vehicles were about to pass. It didn't seem possible.

The sound of cars braking filled the village of Cottontree.

CHAPTER 3

Tom savoured the picturesque scenery as he took the bridge across the river. He wanted to make the serenity last as these might be his final moments with his wife. Everything would change. The life he thought he knew was due to be reset.

The river ran low, which made the muddy banks on either side appear high and wide as if God had dragged his fingernail through the landscape. On either side of the furrow, quaint stone buildings with thatched roofs perched end to end like something from a postcard or one of those photographs printed on fudge boxes. The grey sky and relentless drizzle only lent to the moody atmosphere and made the village appear sleepy and calm instead of drab and depressing. He supposed it depended on perspective.

Like divorce.

To Sophie, divorce represented a new beginning—life begins at forty and all that—but to Tom, it represented defeat, a waste of everything they'd built over the last twelve years. And he wasn't even the one who'd done anything wrong.

So why was she leaving him?

And why was he letting it happen?

"I'm going to miss you, Soph."

"Tom, don't..."

"I still love you."

"Tom, I don't want to do this. There's nothing left to say."

He took his eyes off the road and looked at her. "How about, 'don't go'!"

"Tom, will you please just—hey, look out!"

Tom shoved his foot on the brake before he even knew what he was trying to avoid, but the urgency in Sophie's voice told him enough to know he needed to stop. Even when the windscreen shattered, he still didn't understand what was happening, but he was aware of his wife—soon to be ex-wife—screaming. The world devolved into screeching tyres and grinding metal, and as his vision whirled, Tom thought he glimpsed a truck with two men inside. Then there was nothing but a low brick wall speeding towards him and everything came to a cold, sudden stop. The Mercedes' bonnet crumpled, and the only thing he saw was a strip of grey sky through the ragged hole where the windscreen had been. Slowly, little by little, the sky tilted away, and a muddy river appeared in its place.

The Mercedes was tipping over the bridge.

A shard of glass had somehow wedged itself beneath Tom's thumbnail, causing him to leak blood everywhere, but no pain arrived. He turned sideways in his seat. "Sophie? Soph! Are you all right?"

She smiled at him—one of her old smiles, full of love and trust—and it lit Tom up inside. But the warmth lasted mere seconds, for what looked to be a shovel had smashed through the windscreen and sliced into her neck. It propped her head against the seat, even as her neck-blood jetted down its shiny, aluminium blade. Tom reached out to her, not knowing what to do, or even what had happened, but needing to touch her and make everything all right. He heard people shouting nearby, but their voices disappeared as another bout of screeching tyres overruled them. Looking past his dying wife, Tom spotted a little yellow car speeding towards him.

※

GWEN SPOTTED THE DANGER IN TIME TO REACT, BUT HER driving instincts were not yet automatic and her foot stamped on the brake only partially. The right side of her shoe re-hit the accelerator, so her little car did not brake hard enough to avoid the

danger. She and her screaming friends skidded towards the crumpled saloon at the exact same time a truck swerved to avoid it from
the other direction. It was a simple question of which vehicle
Gwen would hit first.

It turned out to be both.

Because her first instinct had been to avoid the wreck at the
side of the bridge, Gwen yanked her fuzzy pink steering wheel
towards the centre of the bridge. The oncoming truck head-butted
her little car right in the centre of its passenger door and sent
Stacey sprawling into her. Her friend screamed as blood gushed
from her glass-covered face, and in the backseat, Mia called out for
her mom. Gwen did nothing but hold onto the wheel for dear life.

Her car entered another spin, the massive impact redirecting it
back towards the crumpled saloon perched on the side of the
bridge. In the corner of her eye, Gwen saw the truck cartwheel
over the opposite side of the bridge—part of her thought it was
justice for slamming into her.

The last thing she saw was the driver of the saloon leaning over
and shaking a woman in the passenger seat. He didn't even notice
her car skidding towards his at first, but even if he had, there was
nothing he could have done. The nose of her car struck the saloon
square in its rump, and what followed was a feeling of weightless-
ness that seemed to go on forever.

Gwen wondered if she was dead.

CHAPTER 4

T om found himself in darkness. He could see nothing, hear nothing. And he could not breathe. The harder he sucked, the more his lungs shrivelled. Something engulfed his face, something filling his entire mouth and nostrils and threatening to invade his insides. He tried to move, but couldn't feel himself—couldn't imagine any of his limbs. The feeling was not unlike a dream—a detachment from one's self. But it was not a dream.

It was a nightmare.

His lungs burned, and his mouth and nostrils stretched against the foul substance compacting inside of them. No light, nor sound, would come—only suffocation and oblivion. His mind turned to Sophie, his beautiful wife, her throat torn apart by a shovel. What the hell had happened? What was happening now? All he knew was that it had started with divorce. All the bad things in his life led back to it. What had happened to the future? Houses, cars, holidays—they were supposed to have it all, and enjoy it together. That was why they'd started an accountancy firm—to be together in both work and play. Now he was alone and dying in the dark. Maybe dead already.

How did this happen? Help me. Please help me, God, so that I may help Sophie. She needs me. She is hurt. God, are you there?

"Son, I'm here!"

Is that you, God?

"Son, get your arse over here. Some poor sod's buried in the mud. Help me pull him out."

Tom's head throbbed, and he felt himself spinning—on his way to God; he was sure of it—but then ungentle hands grabbed his arms and tugged him away. He cried out as his wrists twisted behind his back and the foul substance sucked and clung to his face, unwilling to release him without a fight. He had lost all sense of direction, but thought, perhaps, he was rolling onto his side. Worms probed his mouth and nose, digging and squirming towards his brain. His eyes detected a scattering of light, and he wondered if there was still a chance to make it to God. His lungs were empty sacs, so deprived of air that he must be dead.

He yelled in agony, his entire body spasming. Sound came back to the world, dominated by his own roaring gasps for air. He gulped, bellowed, and moaned as he doubled-up in pain while rough hands fought to keep him upright. Dirty fingers—those worms—continued probing his mouth, scooping out the foul substance that had nearly suffocated him.

Mud. Wet and disgusting.

"Easy there, mate. Easy! You're okay. Me and my lad have got you."

Son, I'm here. Tom moaned. *Not God. Just a man.*

"W-what happened?"

"We've been in a crash," came a younger male voice, cracked and anxious.

"But you're all right, mate," said the older male voice. "Everything's fine."

Tom tried to get up, but the rough hands kept fighting him. He kicked out defiantly, but felt like a helpless child. "My wife! Sophie! Sophie needs me. She's hur-"

"Tom? I'm over here!"

Tom fought off the strangers enough to sit up. He studied them both and saw the mud-streaked faces of a wiry, blonde teenager and a portly, balding man who resembled the son only in the eyes—a striking sage for both. Tom was interested in neither and looked past them as he searched desperately for his wife.

Ex-wife.

Not yet.

Sophie clutched the side of her head as she staggered towards him, and every few steps she would slip and stumble as her foot connected with a patch of thick, black sludge. The mud covered everything and stole all colour away.

Eventually, Sophie made it over to Tom and dropped to her knees beside him, throwing both arms around his shoulders. He was still wheezing and lightheaded, but he felt his strength return as her warm body pressed against his. It had been a long time since they'd held one another.

I thought you were dead, Soph.

"How...?" he asked, not daring to release her. "How are you okay?"

"We crashed off the bridge," she said. "I blacked out when we hit, but I'm okay, I think. Are you okay?"

"I... I think so."

She broke away from the hug and looked at him. "We're so lucky. Jesus, Tom, we could've died."

We did, he thought to himself, picturing the shovel through her neck. Had he gone crazy? Having just survived a car wreck, it would be no surprise.

"My son and I are okay, too," said the portly man, hiking up his grubby jeans. "Bleeding miracle none of us are hurt."

Tom tried to get his thoughts in order, but all he could summon was an ache in his temples. "What caused the crash? I... I don't remember."

The kid went to speak, but the father cut him off. "Our truck blew a tyre. Must have been something on the bridge. I tried to stop, but it all happened too fast. Any other road and we'd have ended up safely in the ditch. Bloody bridge!"

Tom blinked but continued to see only black sludge. "We're on the river bed?"

The portly man nodded. "Probably what saved us. This river bed is softer than a mattress."

Something didn't feel right. Tom climbed up to his feet. The two strangers attempted to stop him, but he waved them off. "Take it easy, Tom," said Sophie, putting a hand on his back.

"I'm fine. I nearly wasn't, but these men helped me. Thank you. I'm Tom Sumner, and this is my wife, Sophie."

Sophie didn't correct him about their impending divorce, but she gave him an uncomfortable stare. The four of them shook hands.

"I'm Patrick," said the portly man, offering a calloused hand. "This is my lad, Brandon."

"Hello," said Brandon. He nodded at Tom. "You were face-down and out, mate. Wonder how much longer you would have lasted?"

Tom frowned. "Yeah, well, thanks again. I must've been thrown from my car."

"Us too," said Brandon. "I think."

Tom put his finger on one of the many things confusing him. "We were all thrown from our vehicles? Okay, say I accept that, then where are they? Where's my car? Where's your truck?"

Patrick turned and pointed a finger, but his arm fell back to his side and he frowned. "Well, how about that? Can't say I have any sodding idea." He turned to his son. "Bran, did you see our truck?"

Brandon shook his head.

"That's not the only thing that makes no sense," said Tom. "There was water when we crossed the bridge. Now there's only mud."

"He's right," said Brandon. "There was water in the river. Where's it gone?"

Patrick folded his meaty forearms over the top of his protruding belly and shrugged. "It ain't rained in a month. The river's not much more than a puddle. Sure there'll be water further downstream."

Tom sighed. "Fair enough. Let's find our vehicles."

Brandon glanced at Sophie. "Maybe we should just stay here and wait for help?"

Sophie shrugged. "The nearest fire station is a town over, but if I remember this village right, every man, woman, and dog will be gathered around soon. No better spectator sport than an accident."

Patrick examined her, a little leeringly for Tom's liking. "You're from Cottontree, luv? Can't say I've seen you."

"I grew up here. It's been a while."

"Who're your family?"

Sophie ignored the question and walked away. She lifted her knees high to avoid her shoes getting sucked into the mud. It would have been comical any other time—her waddling like a duck. Dizziness tried to claim Tom, but he shook it off and gave pursuit, walking in much the same way.

"Wait up!" shouted Brandon. "We should stick together."

"Then come on," said Sophie. "Let's go."

The four of them traversed the swampy riverbed in loose formation. Tom sought to walk side by side with Sophie, but she kept picking up pace and leaving him behind. Eventually, he gave up and his mind turned, once again, to her torn-open throat. Had he imagined the entire thing? He turned to Brandon. "What do you and your dad do?"

"We're handymen."

"General builders," his father corrected. "We do a lot of work for the village council, the church, other businesses around here."

Tom nodded. "I wish I was handy. Last year, I tried to tile our bathroom floor—half the tiles were cracked by the time I'd finished."

Brandon smiled. "I hate tiling, too. Takes forever."

"It's a piece of piss," said Patrick. "Long as you don't rush the job. Give us a call next time, mate, and I'll do it properly for you."

Tom sniffed. Mud still clogged his airways, and he spat a wad of it onto the ground. He found Patrick coarse, so he maintained conversation with his son. "You worked for your dad long?"

"Almost a year. He's training me up so I can take over the business one day."

"You enjoy it?"

He shrugged. "There are worse jobs. Depends on the task. I like that every day is different. Today we've been digging, but tomorrow we might be cutting timbers for a roof, and power tools are awesome. Once, I used a circular saw on a turkey for a laugh. You should have seen—"

"Digging?" asked Tom. "Do you have shovels on your truck?"

Brandon seemed to flinch at the question, which was odd.

"We have every tool under the son," Patrick butted in. "Couldn't be a builder without them."

Tom nodded. "Of course."

They carried on walking. Sophie was still ahead and rotating her head back and forth like an owl. "Any sign of our car?" Tom asked her.

"Not yet. My watch has stopped working, but I know we've been walking for at least five minutes and I haven't seen a thing. Something doesn't add up. Am I being stupid?"

She wasn't. Tom looked ahead and behind, and all he could see was an endless stretch of swampy, black mud in both directions. Where was the bridge? If they had gone over the low stone wall, surely they would have ended up underneath it, or at least close by. And why wasn't his watch working either?

The situation was, for obvious reasons, unnerving—it wasn't every day you got in a car accident—but the more time that passed, the more it felt like they were in the middle of some bizarre crisis. Nobody voiced their fears, not yet, but Tom could see the trembling of jaws and the rapid blinking of eyes.

Tension filled the air.

"This bleedin' swamp is wearing me out," said Patrick, sluggishly pulling his boots in and out of the mud.

"Me too," said Tom, feeling the onset of a nasty stitch beneath his ribs.

Sophie stopped walking, which caused the entire group to do the same. She crossed her arms and shook her head. "Something is wrong here. We should've stumbled on something by now. I feel like this riverbed doesn't end. We keep walking and walking and walking."

"Stay calm, Soph. It'll be okay." Tom could see her getting frustrated. He was surprised she'd remained calm this long. It was her short temper that had caused her leave of absence from the firm. No good for the staff to be around such anger. A court case was inevitable. When had she become such an angry person? Had it been a gradual change, or a sudden one.

"I'm climbing the bank." she said. "We could have internal injuries or concussion, and it's pretty clear we're not walking towards any help. I feel like we're walking away from it, in fact."

Patrick rubbed his thick hands together with a clap. "All right, luv, after you."

Sophie didn't wait for a consensus, and she stomped through the mud towards the nearest embankment. The distant rumble of thunder seemed to sound as a warning, but she was undeterred. That it was no longer raining, when it had been before the crash, was just another thing unsettling to Tom.

"It's pretty high up," he said, as he approached the bank and stared up the uneven incline. Had the banks seemed so high before?

"It's fine," she replied. "Not that steep at all."

"Looks bloody steep enough to me, luv," said Patrick, staring up the hill with his hands on his hips. Tom imagined it was the same stance he used when he was quoting a job.

"I can make it," said Brandon. "Sophie and I can get to the top and find help if you and Tom want to stay here."

Tom grunted. "I can make it, kid, don't worry about me."

"Sorry, I was just offering to go. I'm younger, that's all."

"We all go," said Sophie. "It's not that steep." Done talking, she climbed up onto the bank, leaning forwards and progressing on her hands and knees.

"Not steep, my arse," said Patrick, cursing a few more times before starting his own climb. He huffed and puffed immediately, which made Tom wonder how the guy coped as a builder—probably by making his son do all the labour.

Tom clambered up onto the slope and, like the others, was forced to use both his hands and feet. The mud of the embankment was firmer than the riverbed, but still wet and loose. Clumps of grass and small rocks came away in his fingernails and caused him mild discomfort as he pulled himself higher. The grey sky threatened to unleash a torrent upon them at any moment, and he panicked about getting stuck halfway up—his arms frozen from fatigue.

Thunder boomed again.

Sophie had already climbed eight feet and showed no sign of slowing down. What had got into her? They were all anxious, of course, but Sophie was acting like her feet were on fire. "Soph, be careful. You're going too fast."

"Not fast enough," she shouted back. "I need to get out of this goddamn ditch."

Patrick grumbled from lower down the slope. "Worry about yourself, mate. Your lass seems steady enough to me."

"I'm not his lass!"

Patrick chuckled between huffing breaths. "Did I hit a sore spot?"

Tom glared. "None of your business. Concentrate on climbing."

"That's what I'm doing, mate. It's you what's holding up the line."

Cursing beneath his breath, Tom dug his hands into the mud and propelled himself upward, determined to catch Sophie. Now, just like her, he wanted nothing more than to get out of this mud-filled ditch. He gritted his teeth and climbed faster and faster, hoisting one leg after another, shoes sinking deeper and deeper into the muddy bank. Within a minute, he was right up alongside his soon-to-be ex-wife. "Reminds me of when we used to jog together, huh? Why did we give that up?"

"I'm not in the mood to reminisce, Tom."

"No, I suppose not."

No longer in the lead, she let up a little, which allowed him to reduce his own pace. He felt sweat on his lower back, icy beneath his buttoned shirt, and had now fully earned that stitch beneath his ribs. Having almost suffocated twenty minutes ago, it'd perhaps not been the best idea to get into a race. Patrick and Brandon were way behind them.

Brandon apparently took it as humiliation because he began sprinting up the hill. Tom wondered if he was trying to impress Sophie.

She's twice your age, kid. Even if she doesn't look it.

Sophie caught a second wind and moved ahead again. Despite how far they'd come, there was a long way to go. The top still seemed miles away, almost unreachable, and Tom was too beat to keep up with Sophie any longer, so instead he tried to reign her in. "Soph! Slow down."

"Stop telling me what to do, Tom. Just sto—"

She yelped as her foot slipped in a slurry of mud and rock. As if attached via some invisible web, the entire patch of embankment gave way beneath her and moved.

"Sophie! Hold on!"

She glared back defiantly, but he had loved her long enough to recognise the glint of fear in her hazel brown eyes. "It's fine," she said unconvincingly. "I'm nearly at the top."

"No, you're not! The top is still far away. Look!"

She did as he asked and looked upwards. "It makes no sense. Where is everyone? Where is help? Why can't I climb out of this goddamn riverbed?"

The ground shifted again, and she slid back two feet, belly flat against the earth. She whimpered, but caught the noise quickly enough that it was barely noticeable.

"Hold on, Soph. Just stay where you are."

"No. I'm getting out of here!"

There was a pained screech, but it didn't come from Sophie. Tom peered down and saw Brandon struggling to hold on. The kid's one hand waved manically in the air as he tried to regain his grip. The bank shifted again, a great clump of earth coming loose like a tectonic plate. Brandon had made up a decent amount of ground on Tom and Sophie, but now he was going in the other direction.

Patrick shouted up to his son. "Watch yourself, you bleedin' idiot."

"Dad! I can't hold on."

"Stop messing around."

"Dad!"

Sophie slipped again. Her body slid through the mud like a sledge, and a second later, she collided with Tom and took him for a ride.

Brandon continued screaming.

Patrick swore.

The entire bank shifted. Tom tried to grab hold, but his fingers penetrated the thick quagmire as if it were no more than spoiled milk. Sophie lay beneath him, clinging for dear life as they descended. "Don't let go, Soph," he urged her, not that she showed any intention.

They picked up more speed, the loose mud moving rapidly. Tom could still hear Brandon's screams, but couldn't control his slide enough to look out for him. His forearm slid over something sharp and he heard himself crying out too, but mostly he was caught in a whirlwind of silent confusion. Seconds passed, and he prayed for the moment to end. To fall without restraint was a terrifying thing.

Then, he felt gravity level out, and realised they were nearing the bottom of the slope. He clutched Sophie tightly and waited for some kind of impact, but instead they came to a gentle stop. He and Sophie lay there, staring at one another in silence. Was it over? Had their fall ended with them still in one piece? If so, then why was there still so much screaming?

With all the craziness of the last hour, he didn't want to endure any more. He felt good right where he was, lying still and looking into Sophie's eyes without her looking away. In her fear, she had forgotten how much she couldn't stand him.

The moment faded, and Sophie wriggled out from underneath him. She climbed to her feet, and when Tom went after her he spotted Brandon lying in the mud with his father kneeling over him.

"Brandon, are you okay?" Sophie asked, hurrying over.

The lad clutched his leg and wailed.

Tom closed the distance to get a closer look. Brandon was in a bad way. A bone stuck out of his shin like a lever, and something else was embedded in the side of his thigh. Combined, the two wounds were a horrible mess. "Oh shit!"

"Help him," Patrick demanded.

Tom frowned. "How? We're not doctors. We're accountants."

"The ground moved," Brandon cried out. "One second it was there, the next it was slipping through my fingers. Help me!"

"What's that stuck in his leg?" said Sophie, cringing as she pointed to the object in his thigh.

Tom got down in the mud and examined Brandon. The break in his shin was bad, and years of watching television told him they needed to press down and pop the bone back into place. No way was he going to be the one to do it though.

"Help him," Patrick demanded again. "Pull that thing out of his leg."

Tom wasn't about to mess with the kid's broken leg, but he could agree to do at least that much. His hands shook, but he was able to get a firm hold on the object sticking out of Brandon's thigh. He readied himself to pull it out.

Brandon mewed. His father fought to hold him still.

"Do it quickly!" Sophie urged.

Tom considered counting to three, but instead just went for it. He yanked the object out in one pull. It had not been as deeply embedded as he'd expected. As a consequence, he toppled backwards with unexpected momentum, but managed to retain the object in his hand. It was covered in blood but white underneath.

"Oh my God," said Sophie. "Is that...?"

Tom nodded. "It's a bone."

"I need to get a tetanus," said Brandon, gritting his teeth and attempting to laugh. It didn't work because a moment later his head fell back in the mud and he passed out.

Patrick slapped his son's cheeks, cursing and trying to wake him up. Sophie stood silently in a daze, but Tom was still on high alert. He checked the back of his arm, remembering the pain he'd felt as he'd slid down the embankment, and there he discovered a deep, bleeding wound.

What had sliced him? He glanced back at the muddy slope and saw chalky mounds weeping up to the surface, emerging like whiteheads on greasy skin.

"The river's full of bones," he said, wondering when he had lost his mind.

CHAPTER 5

"What do we do? What do we do?" Patrick kept asking it over and over. Brandon was still unconscious, and his father had lost sight of anything else. Even when Tom pointed out the bones emerging from the muddy embankments, the builder never took his eyes off his son.

"I think we need to see to his leg," said Tom, deciding to focus on one thing at a time. "We can't leave the bone sticking out like that."

"Why hasn't anyone come to help us?" Sophie said, more to herself than anybody else. She was rubbing at her throat and wincing. "What's happening?"

Tom knelt in front of Patrick, Brandon lying between them. "Patrick? We need to set Brandon's leg, okay? I'm not a doctor, but I'm pretty sure we need to get his bone back, more or less, where it's supposed to be. Heck, I don't know, but I think I'm right."

Patrick stared at him and blinked like a computer in his brain was restarting, but then gave a firm nod. "What do I need to do?"

Tom swallowed. His throat was dry. "I think... I think you put one hand on top of the other and push down with all your weight. You need to push the bone back into place."

Patrick nodded again. His demeanour had changed, a robot awaiting commands. A way of coping, perhaps? The father put one hand on top of the other and positioned his palms over his son's protruding bone.

"Okay, Patrick, I'll count to three. You ready?"

Patrick gave a robotic nod.

"One... two..."

Tom swallowed the lump in his throat.

"Three!"

Patrick pressed down with all his ample weight. A gruesome clicking sound echoed off the banks, followed by a deafening silence. Brandon shifted, but remained asleep. Tom couldn't see what had happened because Patrick had frozen with his hands over the wound.

"Okay, Patrick. Good job. Slowly move your hands away."

This time, the father did not obey. His lip quivered, and he kept squinting as if a fly had landed in his eye. "Patrick? It's okay. Let's have a look."

He got a hold of himself and nodded, but the robotic calm had evaporated. Moving in millimetres, he took his hands away from his son's leg.

Tom sighed.

Brandon's bone no longer jutted out of his shin. His leg was drenched in blood, but there didn't seem to be any fresh liquid spurting. While Tom had no clue if they'd made things better or worse, they did at least appear less gruesome.

"I think you got it, Patrick. Good job."

Patrick's throat bulged, and he looked like he might be sick. "I'm not usually such a piss-soaked blanket. It's just..."

Tom patted his arm. "It's your son. I get it. Parents are supposed to fall apart when their kids are hurt. It's the normal thing to do."

Patrick sniffed back snot, ending any chance he might cry, and nodded toward Sophie who had edged away from the gory scene. "You two have children?"

"No," Tom replied, watching Sophie take deep breaths a few yards away. "We never had any."

"You're lucky. You think Bran's leg will heal from this?"

"I don't know, Patrick. I wish I could be more help. Like I said, I'm an accountant."

"Least you're not a solicitor, I suppose. Things are a bloody mess. Some father I am, letting my lad get hurt like this."

Tom sighed. "This wasn't your fault, Patrick. We'll figure everything out, I promise."

They were destined for a newspaper headline was Tom's true opinion—he just hoped their story wouldn't end with a tragic punch-line.

Please, let us be in some ridiculous situation we'll laugh about later. Group crashes off bridge and wanders around abandoned marshland for 3 days. Found safe by milkman.

But somehow that headline didn't seem right. It didn't explain the bones in the ground or the shifting earth. Tom felt the riverbed might split apart at any moment and swallow him whole.

"Hey," said Sophie, stomping through the mud back towards them. She was still rubbing at her throat gingerly. "I think I see something ahead. It's far, but..."

Tom leapt up, leaving Patrick with his son. "What is it?"

"Look down the riverbed as far as you can. I'm sure I can see something."

Tom cupped a hand over his brow and squinted, examining the horizon for a good half-a-minute before reaching a conclusion. "I think you're right. The riverbed drops, but I think I see the top of something poking out of the dip. Maybe it's Patrick's truck. It might even be the bridge."

"The bridge is in the centre of the village," said Sophie, sounding relieved. "There'll be people there for sure."

"If the bridge is downriver, how did we end up way back here?" asked Patrick. He still knelt beside his son, stroking his glistening forehead.

"There are things about this situation," said Sophie, "that I don't think we'll understand until much later. Until then, let's focus on getting out of this riverbed and nothing else."

Patrick's bushy eyebrows lowered like a bear about to fend off an attack. "What do we do about Bran?"

"You'll have to stay here with him," said Sophie. "As long as Tom and I find help, everything will work out fine."

Patrick gazed up at the grey sky and seemed to think for a

moment. When he lowered his gaze again, he looked at Tom and not Sophie. "It's getting dark. You can't hang about."

"We won't," said Tom. "We'll get Brandon some help as our first priority. He's the only one injured." *Unless you count my wife's throat being torn open,* he thought.

Patrick said nothing else, and the moment stretched so long that Sophie asked him what he was staring at. He blinked and shook his head. "Nothing. It's just, I had a feeling for a second that there was another car involved in the accident."

"It's a blur for me too," Tom admitted. "But I don't remember another car."

Patrick shrugged. "Maybe my brain took a knock."

"You feel okay for us to leave you and Brandon?"

"Don't see what other choice there is. Don't bloody well like it, but I see no other way of getting Bran help. So get moving!"

Tom said okay, and was about to raise a hand to wave when he realised it would be stupid. So he turned and left Patrick and Brandon behind without a word. Ironically, now he had sighted something in the distance, he felt even more panicked. The situation had been unsettling, verging on traumatic, and the thought of imminent rescue agitated him. He had to force himself not to go running off like a terrified child, pleading for help at the top of his lungs. If Sophie wasn't walking beside him, he might have.

"You okay?" he asked her, wanting to reach out and take her hand, but knowing what the result would be.

She exhaled loudly and kept her eyes forward. "What do you fucking think?"

Tom's nerves were fried, so he resisted the urge to snap back at her. Sophie's combative stance towards him was grating, but there was nothing to gain from an argument. "Soph, can we maybe put the divorce on hold for now? I know we're not the best of friends, but we're in a bit of a hole—literally. I'm anxious, you're anxious, we should try to remember we've been husband and wife for a decade. So please, no more blowing hot and cold."

She huffed and turned to him with yet more scorn, but then she softened. "You're right. I'm sorry. It's not you, Tom, it's this village. I hate Cottontree. The car crash, this weird ditch... It feels like one cosmic joke at my expense. Like Cottontree is poking a finger at me and saying, 'nah nah, you came back!'"

"It's a place, not a person, Soph. We could have crashed anywhere."

"But we didn't! We crashed in the shit hole I ran away from twenty years ago."

Tom had rarely seen her so irrational, even during the breakup of their marriage, which had involved much in the way of hysteria. "Cottontree seems beautiful to me," he said cautiously. "What happened to make you hate the place so much? You've never spoken much about your childhood."

Instead of giving an answer, she ignored the question altogether, folding her arms as she walked away.

It made sense really. She had not shared stories of her childhood during their marriage, so she wasn't about to do it now that they were separating.

"I'm sorry, Soph. Today was going to be shit no matter what, but I never expected it to be this bad. I'm sorry I crashed the car."

"It wasn't your fault, Tom."

He frowned. Defending him wasn't one of her hobbies lately, so it took him by surprise. "How do you know it wasn't?"

"It just wasn't! My memory is a blur like yours, but I'm sure it wasn't your fault. It was Cottontree."

Now he understood her defence of him. It wasn't that she was defending him, but that she hated the village more than she hated him. He had gained her loyalty by default.

Is that right? Does she hate me now?

Does Soph hate me?

The thought crippled Tom like a punch to the ribs. Hard enough coming to terms with the fact he might not be living with her any longer, but the thought she might actually hate him? That left him feeling sick to his bones. He couldn't think about it for a single second. "What do you mean, it was Cottontree that caused the crash?"

She shook her head. "Never mind, I'm just angry and I feel shit. This place has a way of kicking you when you're down. Nothing good ever happens here. Shit, I wish I had my cigarettes."

He frowned at her. "You're smoking again?"

She pulled out a silver Zippo lighter. "Been a stressful few weeks. Whatever gets me through till the end, you know?"

"Suppose it's not my place to judge anymore. I understand what you mean, anyway. Last thing you and I needed today was—"

"Quiet! Look!" She pointed ahead and picked up pace. He did his best to keep up. Ahead, the riverbed declined abruptly into a sink hole. When the river was high, the massive depression would be an invisible secret beneath the water, but with the riverbed dried up, it was naked and exposed. Soph stood at the edge, at the point where the ground fell away in a precipice.

Tom kept blinking because he was sure his eyes were deceiving him. No other explanation.

"You see that too, right?" asked Soph after a lengthy silence.

He nodded. "I don't understand it, but I see it."

Sitting right in the centre of the circular depression was a house. And beside that house was a burnt, blackened oak tree.

֍

PATRICK SAT IN THE MUD BESIDE HIS SON AND TRIED TO MAKE sense of the last hour. He was not a man who believed in the supernatural, or even the unexplained. His world was, for the most part, modest and mapped out—good ale and bad ale, good pies and bad pies, exciting football and boring work. As far as lives went, his was uninspired, and he knew it. He accepted that his limitations prevented him from anything greater, and to struggle against his shortcomings would only have left him resentful and unfulfilled. So, a long time ago, when his school work was lacking and his manners were poor, he decided to accept his lot in life. A man had to gain happiness from what he had and enjoy the more easily attainable things in life. Like having a son.

Brandon wasn't much like his dad, which was probably a good thing. He cared little about sport, despite Patrick's best attempts to get him interested, and wasn't much of a barfly either. If left alone, Brandon would spend most of his time in his room, doing things better left unseen. A typical teenager, Patrick supposed, but he still paused from time to time to worry. Bringing Bran into the family business was a way of keeping a closer eye on the boy, and maybe even bringing him out of his shell. It had appeared to be working lately, and some of the lads even liked Brandon. Most still didn't though.

Brandon was odd.

But he's still my son.

Brandon had been mumbling and fidgeting during the last few minutes, and Patrick hoped he might wake up, and that he wouldn't be in too much pain. The sight of his leg had been hard to bear. His broken bone sticking out like that...

His ma's gunna kill me.

It was the shock of Bran's injury that had blinded him to what was going on around him, but in the last ten minutes it had seeped in gradually. The riverbed bled bones like a scene from a horror movie, and even now, only a yard away, he spotted a grinning skull rising from the mud. It wasn't human, mercifully, and resembled a large rodent, or perhaps a badger—something with large front teeth. The embankment on either side of him oozed yet more bones, reminding him of one time when he had squeezed a massive build-up of tophi from his thumb during a bad case of gout. Brandon had gagged at the time, and it was hardly surprising. Patrick felt a little nauseous himself right now just thinking about it. Or maybe it was his present situation.

He stroked Bran's forehead, clammy and hot. Could you get a fever from a broken bone? Tom had seemed confident they'd needed to set the bone back in place, but he had also admitted he didn't know what he was doing for sure. Had they made the injury worse by interfering? What if Brand ended up losing his leg —or worse?

Don't you die on me, son. I'll bloody well kill you!

Strange, but what Patrick wanted more than anything was Brandon's ma. He was the man of the house, but when it came to blood and guts, she was the no-nonsense one. She'd take care of their boy while Patrick removed himself to the sitting room.

Brandon opened his eyes.

"Bran, you're awake!"

Brandon didn't react to his father's voice or respond in any way. He stared up from on his back, focused only on the grey sky. His mouth opened, wider and wider, and his throat became a gaping hole.

"Bran, calm down. Everything's okay!"

Brandon bolted upright into a sitting position like a mannequin pulled up on strings. His jaw clamped shut and blood spurted from between his lips. Patrick watched in horror as a morsel of flesh slithered down his son's chin. He had bitten off the tip of his tongue. Stunned into inaction, Patrick was powerless to help his son. He sat there in the mud, staring.

Brandon's vacant stare locked on his father, and he grinned, working his mouth hungrily as more blood spilled down his chin. Then, in a cracked and wispy voice, he said: "She'll never let us leave."

Patrick stammered. "W-who won't?"

But rather than answer, Brandon threw himself back down in the mud. His eyes closed, and he went back to sleep.

CHAPTER 6

"What's a house doing here?" Tom still couldn't believe it. "A house!"

Sophie had no answers. What explanation could there be for a house at the bottom of a riverbed? The building didn't even appear weathered, showing no signs it had ever existed underwater—just a well-kept cottage as long as it was wide. A tiny front door marked its centre, and six small windows—three to either side—sat beneath a sloped thatch roof. Net curtains obscured any opportunity to see inside, but Tom thought he saw a shadow move behind one of them.

"This is all a dream," he said. "This place does not exist."

"It's right there," said Sophie. "We're staring at it."

"But..." He put both hands to his head and pulled clumps of hair like a mad man. "It makes no sense. Is this a local landmark or something? Do you know what this place is?"

"No," said Sophie. "My entire childhood, I don't remember the river ever drying up. I remember boats and people fishing but never this."

"Then how can a house be here?"

She thought for a moment, squeezing the tip of her nose like she did whenever she worked out sums in her head. "The river never used to run through here," she said. "I remember a school trip to the local abbey. They taught us that the Church dug a bifurcation to divert part of a nearby river through a tiny hamlet in the Thirteenth century that eventually became Cottontree. It helped the farms around the abbey thrive for a while until it was abandoned. Maybe this house got swallowed up when they redirected the river."

That's what it seemed like—like the house had been built in the path of a surging river, enveloped and devoured by its rushing waters. Except... "This place doesn't look like it's ever seen water, nor does it look hundreds of years old. The roof is bone dry, and the stone walls are bare. Wouldn't they be plastered in green stuff? When we watched that series about deep sea divers, the shipwrecks were always covered in fuzz—algae or whatever."

"What do you want me to say, Tom? I have no idea why there's a fucking cottage sat at the bottom of an empty river. Or why there's a dead oak tree next to it. Perhaps we died in the crash and went to Hell. God knows, it wouldn't surprise me."

"What are you talking about, Soph? You're saying we deserve to go to Hell? For what? Getting a divorce? Or the fact that you cheated on me? Gee, I'm so glad I get to burn right alongside you, even though I'm innocent!"

She thrust a finger in his face. "Yes, I cheated. What a filthy fucking whore I am! But you're not innocent, believe me. I never would've done it when we first got married. You were a different person then. We were so in love."

"I still love you, Soph," he grunted.

"No... No, you blame me." She rubbed at her throat and closed her eyes. "You can't love someone when you blame them for everything wrong in your life."

"The only thing wrong in my life is that my wife wants a divorce."

She sneered in that way he hated—so angry and dismissive. "No," she said. "You hate that we haven't been able to build an accounting empire, and that your house is smaller than the one next door. You're never happy, Tom. You always want more. When we were younger, that was okay because we still had time. Now time's run out, and you haven't won the game you've been playing with the universe. You blame me for not working hard enough, for wanting holidays and nights out instead of investments and savings. You blame me for—"

"Bullshit! Don't scapegoat me for your shitty behaviour, Soph. Yes, I want more. More for us! I've worked my arse off for the both of us!"

"And how resentful you are that I refused to work sixty hours a week alongside you. What's the point, Tom? What's it all for? We're not happy."

He gritted his teeth and tried to stop the anger spilling out of his mouth, but it was hopeless. "I don't know, Soph! Maybe I thought it would be for our kids."

"And there it is! The real reason you hate me!"

"I love you!"

"No, you don't. And I don't love you. Not anymore."

Tom clutched his stomach and gasped. The last thing he wanted to do was cry in front of her, but the tears would not be stopped, and they came with gusto. Sophie shook her head and rolled her eyes as though she thought he was playing the sympathy card, and he should've been angry about it, but the fight had left him. He collapsed into the mud, fingers sinking into the black slime.

"Look," said Sophie, a hint of compassion creeping back into her voice. "It doesn't matter anymore. It doesn't matter who's wrong and who's right. We both deserve to be happy. It doesn't have to be together. I hope one day you get what you want, Tom— or at least settle for what you have."

Tom said nothing. He didn't want her pity. In fact, he hated that he was in any way pitiable. What had happened to the man he used to be? Soph was right, he never was happy—and it wasn't because he had nothing to be happy about. As far as things went, life was good. It just wasn't great. There was something missing. A gaping hole.

They both knew what it was.

"Come on," said Sophie, offering him a hand. "I know it sounds crazy, but we should go knock on the front door."

He looked up at her from the mud. "What?"

"We still need to get off this riverbed, don't we? We walked this way looking for help. Well, we found a house."

"You don't actually think anyone lives here, do you?"

She shrugged. "A family of fish people?"

The absurdity of it pierced Tom's misery, and he exploded with laughter. He took Sophie's hand and allowed her to pull him up. "Maybe there's a little old lady shacked up with a lobster and a brood of lobster children."

"And don't forget Uncle Swordfish."

Tom laughed louder and had to catch his breath. "Yeah, that guy's real fishy."

Sophie cackled louder, and for a moment, they were husband and wife again—laughing about ridiculous things to break the tension. "So, is that a yay or a nay on paying a house call to the fish people?"

Tom stared at the strange old cottage and couldn't find a reason to say no. There seemed to be nothing else on the riverbed, which made exploring the house seem inevitable rather than optional. "It's absurd," he said, "but what else can we do but check this place out? Just so you understand though, I am choosing to do this through sheer lack of other options." He put his hand out to her and smiled. "It's slippery."

Sophie stared at him for a moment but took his hand without comment. They sidled down the slope together, moving on a diagonal rather than straight forward and risk picking up too much speed. The last thing they needed was a headlong tumble down a fifteen-foot slope—Brandon was testament to that.

Again, Tom thought he saw a shadow flit past one of the windows, and his heartbeat got its tracksuit on. He tried not to let his mind get carried away with implications and just focus on the information in front of him. Adding his own context would be bad. Context made things appear better or worse, and an accountant should only be interested in what is. He was alive and unhurt, about to knock on a front door. That was all.

Sophie lost her footing and Tom had to keep her from falling. She righted herself without too much trouble, but only thanks to his help. She gave him a nod. "Cheers."

"You're welcome. Sorry about your shoes."

"Not even sure I'm still wearing any," she said. "They might have fallen off an hour ago, and I wouldn't know it in all this mud."

"It stinks as well," said Tom, wrinkling his nose. "Worse here than where we woke up."

Sophie wrinkled her nose too. "It's like... rotten eggs."

"Not you, is it?"

"Cheeky bastard!"

They were both smiling when they reached the bottom of the slope, but the levity ended as soon as they faced the house in front of them. There was nothing overtly sinister about it, aside from its location, but there was no way it should feasibly exist. Anywhere else in rural Cottontree and it might have appeared normal, but houses did not belong on riverbeds—and nor did the creepy-looking tree listing beside it. It had no leaves, only blackened, twisted branches.

"More bones," said Sophie, nodding towards the ground. The mud was thick with them—small bones, long bones, oddly shaped bones. A graveyard.

Tom let go of Sophie's hand and strolled forwards. "Maybe this is a nuclear testing site, and a family of mutants have made their home here."

She raised an eyebrow at him. "I thought I married an accountant, not a comic book writer."

"Better luck next time," he said, moving away and placing himself between her and the house. Maybe it was a genetic hangover of his gender, or perhaps he still loved her enough to care, but he was suddenly concerned for her safety. It dawned on him they might be screwed, even if he didn't understand why. Who knew what they would find inside this weird old house?

He stepped forward and knocked on the door.

He had not been expecting it to open.

Or for a woman to greet him.

CHAPTER 7

"H-hello? I... we..." Tom didn't know what to say. The young woman was beautiful and fair, with blonde hair spilling over her shoulders and down the front of her old-fashioned viridian dress. She smiled kindly, and her eyes brimmed with understanding, but were of no discernible colour. "Please," she said. "Both come in."

Sophie stood behind Tom, and he felt her clutch the back of his arm as he returned the odd woman's smile. He fidgeted like there were maggots on his skin. "W-Who are you?"

"A rude question to ask at my door. I am Emily Tanner."

"I'm sorry to intrude. My name is Thomas Sumner, and this is my wi... this is Sophie."

"It is a pleasure to meet you both, but please let us go inside. It is not safe out here."

Sophie stepped up beside Tom. "Why isn't it safe?"

The odd woman opened her door wider. "Please?"

Tom wanted to turn and run, but told himself not to be silly. What was there to be afraid of?

Emily Tanner remained in the open doorway. Eventually they both went inside. Tom glanced left and right, half-expecting monsters to jump out, but all he saw was a sparse, yet cosy living room with two wooden chairs and a well-worn rocking chair on a stone floor. At the rear of the room, a fireplace drew the eye but was not lit.

"You have a lovely home," said Sophie.

Tom cleared his throat. "Er, yes... a lovely home. You live here alone, Emily?"

"Since my husband's departure, yes. A quiet existence, I admit. Rarely do I receive guests like this, but it's always a pleasure. How did you come to be here?"

"We were in a car crash," Tom explained. "Up on the bridge."

Emily stared at them for a few moments until a polite smile grew upon her lips. "That bridge is so awfully narrow—barely wide enough to get a horse and cart across. People are so often encountering folly there. The abbot promised to have a new one built, but nothing moves with haste when it comes to the Church—except collecting tithes, that is." She squawked with what must have been laughter. It led her to cover her mouth. "Pardon my blasphemy."

"You said it wasn't safe outside," said Sophie. "What did you mean?"

Emily's smile melted away. "Have you not see him?"

Tom shook his head. "Seen who?"

"The blind monk."

Tom and Sophie looked at one another, using their years of marriage to communicate wordlessly that this woman was crazy. Emily Tanner acted as though living on a riverbed was normal and now spoke about blind monks and unsubstantiated dangers.

Emily noticed their exchange and frowned at them. "You folks don't believe me? I suppose I shouldn't blame you. This is a strange place for travellers."

"I grew up here," said Sophie.

Emily seemed not to hear. "Please, both of you, take a seat. I shall build us a fire. There's always less reason to fret with warmth in the bones."

Taking a seat that wasn't a pile of mud sounded good to Tom. His body ached, and he was living with the constant tickle of nausea, so he sat down with relief. Sophie was more reluctant, but took the seat next to him. The chairs were solid oak. Emily stacked the fire with dark logs and got a healthy flame flickering within minutes. The woman was delicate, but clearly able. "The blind monk," she said, turning away from the rising fire. "You've not heard of him?"

Sophie shook her head. "No."

"And you grew up here, how strange."

"Who is he?" Tom asked.

Emily placed a metal apparatus over the open fire and produced a small iron pot that she placed inside. Tom deduced she was heating water to make tea. While they waited, she sat down on the rocking chair. "He is a monk, of course, or at least he used to be. The abbot once said the blind monk was the most devout of the monks at the abbey. Obsessed with doing God's work, he spent the days performing exorcisms, prosecuting witches, or flagellating himself whenever he was idle. The monk never allowed himself to rest, nor enjoy pleasure of any kind. If ever his fellow monks tried to convince him to serve the Lord in a less severe way, he would admonish them for their lack of piety. The villagers hated the monk, for whenever he would visit, down from the abbey, he would condemn hard-working people for the slightest of infractions. He once caught the local butcher talking to a woman not his wife. At noon, he whipped the man before the entire village and had the woman's hair cut to the scalp. Soon, married men no longer acknowledged women not their wives, and the village became a fretful place."

"We don't have many monks anymore," said Sophie. "This isn't the Dark Ages."

Emily smiled mirthlessly. "We have few here now also. Only the blind monk."

"How did he go blind?" Tom asked.

"By piercing his own eyes. A madness to us, but to the monk, a way of serving the Lord. His daily bouts of flagellation were not enough, and his compulsion to serve Heaven grew and grew. He believed that witnessing the village's sins was corrupting his own immortal soul—that to look upon sin is to endorse it. One night, alone in the abbey, he took a silver crucifix and heated it in a fire. Once red hot, he popped his own eyeballs until they were grease upon his cheeks. Anyone who reported seeing him after that described a man of pure evil. A local harlot, pregnant with a young lord's baby, was set upon by the monk one night in the church gardens. He tore the foetus from between her legs and left her barren. When she committed suicide a week later, her body was exhumed from its grave and found half-eaten by wolves."

"Enough!" snapped Sophie. "What the fuck is wrong with you?"

Emily stood up from her rocking chair and marched towards Sophie. Tom's legs trembled as he prepared to leap up and block the woman's attack, but she simply turned to the fire and bent over. She used a small metal hook to lift the pot from the flames and took it over to the corner of the room. She came back soon after with two steaming pewter mugs. It wasn't tea inside, but what smelt like lemon.

"I shall help you," said Emily. "Anyone out there, walking the river, is in a lot of trouble, make no mistake—the monk walks the silt, with the bones of his victims rising in his wake."

Tom almost dropped his lemon-water. "What did you say about bones?"

"The bones," Emily repeated. "You know when the blind monk will pay you a visit because the riverbed bleeds bones. His victims."

Tom stared at Sophie and mouthed the words, "Patrick and Brandon."

Emily caught their communication and smiled. "You have friends?"

"Not exactly," said Sophie. "Some people from the crash. One of them is hurt badly. Before we left them alone, there was... a lot of bones."

"Then your friends are already dead. Please, let me take you down to the cellar. It's safe there, and you can rest awhile while I send for help."

Tom noticed a hatch in the middle of the stone floor, covered partially by an old rug. What was down there? Why would it be any safer than in this room?

It became a non-issue because Sophie stood up, her body unfolding like a jack-knife. "What the fuck are you talking about, woman? You're mad. Our friends are not dead, and we don't want to hang out in your shitting basement."

"Do not curse in my home, thank you. My hospitality is not endless, I assure you. Refuse my help and leave if you wish." She flicked her wrist. "Go outside. Take your chances. Regret it."

"We need to call an ambulance," said Tom. "Do you have a telephone? Our friend has broken his leg."

Emily marched to her front door, thick heels clicking on the stone. When she opened it, she stood to one side. "There are no doctors in Abbeydale. The only thing I can offer is warmth beside my fire and a place to rest up in my cellar. Take it if you wish."

Sophie pulled a face. "Abbeydale?"

Emily folded her arms. "Please, leave, unless you are willing to accept the rules of my home."

"Fine," said Sophie, glancing at the floor hatch dismissively as she marched right by it. "Just tell us where the bridge is so we can make our way back to where we crashed."

Emily frowned. "The bridge?"

"Yes, the bridge. We told you that's where we crashed. Where can we find it?"

"Why, it's right outside."

Sophie and Tom exchanged another look. Then Tom marched to the doorway and stuck his head outside. "What the hell?"

The bridge spanned right overhead, smothering the house with its shadow. Sophie stepped beside him and saw for herself. "How did we not see it?"

"Because it wasn't there before," said Tom. He turned on Emily. "What is this place? Where are we?"

"You're in Abbeydale. You folks sure are strange."

Tom huffed. "Yeah, we're the strange ones."

"It's so high up," said Sophie, still staring at the bridge. "It doesn't seem possible."

"Because it's not," said Tom. "None of this is possible. We need to get out of this place."

"You should come inside," said Emily. There was a fearful look about her now, one that made Tom worry far more than all of her earlier warnings.

"We're not coming back inside your home," said Tom. "We're going to get Patrick and Brandon. If you're a good person, you'll help."

Emily's eyes widened, and she took a step back. "Leave my home? I would like to help you, but..."

"Thank you for the tea." said Tom. He passed through her door without looking back and was glad to see Sophie right behind him.

"Mad bitch," she muttered. "She thinks she's living in the past."

Tom looked at her. "What do you mean?"

"She said this is Abbeydale. Abbeydale was the name of the hamlet that eventually grew into Cottontree. There's a street in the village named after it. I forgot the history of why they changed it."

"Maybe Emily's a re-enactor," he suggested. "Like one of those people who play pretend at fetes and stuff."

"Who gives a shit," said Sophie, stomping towards the hill. "She can carry on playing games all by herself."

"Wait! Please wait!" Emily called out to them from the house. She set foot on the soft black mud cautiously as if she worried she might sink beneath its depths. Tom knew the feeling. It seemed she had not been outside in some time, for she shaded her eyes as she looked up at the greying sky as if the sun were blazing down upon them. Only a grey sky hung overhead though, which was strange as it seemed to have been getting dark for over an hour. She took something propped up against the wall beside her front door and brought it over to Tom.

Tom took the wooden broom from her and was confused. "What do I need this for?"

"You said your friend has a broken leg. Not much you can do if rot sets in, but you can at least make a splint for him."

The woman had provided a solution he'd not thought of, so he thanked her. Then he looked up at the looming spectre of the bridge. From its elevated position, it seemed huge—much larger than he remembered it being when he'd driven over it. He thought he could see shapes moving across it back and forth, black blobs stopping periodically like faces looking down. If he looked at it much longer, he'd succumb to fear, so he turned his gaze back to Emily. "This place isn't normal, is it?"

Emily returned a blank stare as if his question had no answer, but after a moment, she tried to provide one. "God provides mystery so we may have something to do. All places are normal to those who live there." She stared down at the ground, next to Tom's feet. "We don't have long to find your friends. It is probably already too late."

Tom saw the bones oozing up out the mud and nodded silently.

৪৯৪৯

BRANDON OPENED HIS EYES AGAIN, BUT THIS TIME HE WAS LUCID. His forehead had cooled in the last twenty minutes and there was no more sweating. Patrick worried both were signs of his son dying, but now he was awake, and he seemed alert.

"Help coming?" he asked around his swollen and bloodied tongue.

Patrick nodded. "Tom and Sophie went to get some. Is the pain bad? You bit off the end of your tongue."

He nodded. "Esh! Is bad."

"I'm sorry, son."

"Ma idot."

Patrick grabbed Brandon's hand and squeezed. "You're not an idiot, son. Not the best climber in the world, granted, but we all slipped. You just slipped a little worse. Trying to impress the woman, huh?"

Brandon turned his head in shame. A trickle of blood spilled down his cheek. The way he blinked so slowly suggested he was in a world of hurt. Patrick's heart ached for him.

"Don't be embarrassed, lad. Wouldn't mind a go at her myself. Think she and her husband are on the bricks, so I'll fight you for her."

"Don't wunna fwight."

Patrick frowned. "Figure of speech."

A pair of tears spilled down Brandon's cheeks. "De cwash was my fwault, wasn't it? I never twied down de swovels."

Patrick put a finger against his son's lips. "Shush, now! Accidents happen. I didn't help things by braking so hard. You just keep quiet about everything. You blacked out and you don't remember a thing, okay?"

"I cwould've kwilled someone."

"But you didn't."

"What bout ovva cwar?"

Patrick frowned. "Other car?"

Brandon propped himself up on his elbows, wincing as his leg moved. He spoke slower, which meant his words slurred a little less. "I didn't remember at first, but now I do. There was a car full of girls. What if they're hurt?"

"Just keep quiet, Brandon. That's an order."

Brandon huffed.

Patrick rubbed at his face, forgetting that his hands were caked in mud. Why didn't his son see he was looking out for him? All he ever did was look out for Brandon—providing for him, teaching him, covering for him. Covering for him was the worst. If his ma knew what he got up to in the wee hours...

Jesus.

Patrick wiped his hands off on his shirt and leant back in the mud. He was exhausted and struggling to hold himself up. When his left hand came down, he swore and gritted his teeth, bringing it back up urgently, bloody and gouged.

"What is it, dad?"

"Don't know." He studied the spot where he'd put his hand and saw a bone—a jawbone complete with teeth. Human teeth. No mistaking it. Patrick threw the bone down in disgust and clambered to his feet. Brandon was unable to get up, so he just stared at his father fearfully.

"Dad?"

The riverbed had been replaced by a field of bones, so many that there was barely space to step and avoid them. Where were they coming from? Bones didn't just seep up from the ground. Human bones.

"We need to get the fuck out of this ditch," said Patrick.

"I can't get up, dad."

Patrick looked down at his injured son and swore again. Truthfully, he didn't know what he would do even if Brandon was on his feet. They had already tried climbing their way out the riverbed, to disastrous results, and Tom and Sophie had set off and were yet to return. That left one option for Patrick—go the opposite way to Tom and Sophie. He imagined doing that, though, only for them to return with help minutes later. No, the best thing would be to stay put as planned.

Movement caught Patrick's eye. He traced it to a pile of bones higher than those surrounding it. Something was disturbing the ground, and as he watched, the movement increased and the bones rattled and knocked together.

Was an animal rooting about? A rat?

No, too big.

"Stay here," he told his son.

"Where else am I going to go?"

Patrick watched his footing as he stepped through the bones, knocking many aside while stepping directly on top of others with his heavy work boots. The smaller ones gave way with a sickening snap and reduced to splinters. He wondered if he had stumbled upon some mass grave from ancient times. They might all become famous. Not with his luck though. Things like that never happened to Patrick Garter.

He was just a few feet away from the writhing mass of bones now. He asked himself what exactly he was expecting to find. Nothing that could help him, that was for sure. It was nothing but a total lack of anything else to do that led him to inspect the movement. Odds were, he would discover some nasty little critter and get bitten.

"What is it, dad?" Bran's words were still mumbled. Would his tongue keep swelling until he choked on it?

"Don't worry, Bran. Just an animal or something." He looked down at the bones, still rattling and hopping, although the movement was less now. *Here goes nothing*, he thought and kicked the bones aside.

A hand burst out of the ground and clasped his ankle, unbalancing him and tripping him to the ground. He spilled amongst the bones, shards digging into his back and shoulders, but he was too consumed by fear to acknowledge the pain. The pile of bones cascaded as something emerged from the earth. The hand still clasped Patrick's ankle tightly, using it as leverage to pull its owner out of the hole. A hole beneath the mud and bones.

Patrick screamed. Brandon screamed too and started begging to know what was wrong. Patrick kicked out, trying to get his ankle free, but he could not shake the hand loose. A body slid out of the hole like a nightmarish mockery of birth. The mud was so viscous it covered the abomination head to toe, clinging to every inch of skin. Patrick saw two stark-white, unblinking eyes staring back at him.

The creature clambered fully from the hole and reached out for Patrick. Brandon was screaming in the background, but beneath it was the sound of moaning—terrified moaning. Those stark-white eyes, staring out through the mud, were wide with fear. The creature wanted help. It dawned on Patrick then what he was really seeing. Not a monster, but a person. It was no demon emerging from the bowels of Hell.

It was a victim.

But of what?

"Fuck me sideways," said Patrick, biting back his fear and taking the frightened stranger in his arms. He forced them down to the ground, and when they stopped resisting, laid them down flat. It was a miracle they hadn't suffocated with so much mud on them —buried in the ground just like Tom had been. What was happening in this goddamn place?

The victim struggled, so Patrick had to shush them constantly. From their slightness and size, he could tell it was a woman—or a girl. He made a start on helping her, first by wiping the mud away from her eyes and nose, and then from her mouth. It was her mouth that made him recoil. She must have seen the shock on his face because she started moaning frantically and trying to get up.

Jesus Christ.

Patrick tried to appear calm. "Just lie still and let me help you." At his back, Brandon demanded answers, but he would have to sit tight. This girl needed Patrick more. He continued scooping mud from her face, ignoring the fact her lips were badly bruised and stitched tightly shut with coarse black thread. As the mud fell away, she revealed herself to be a frightened teenager—beautiful, despite her fear. She couldn't answer him, so it was good fortune that there was a glittering pendant around her neck with a name emblazoned on it. "Everything is going to be okay, Stacey," said Patrick. "Help is on its way."

❧

EMILY COMPLAINED THE ENTIRE TIME, TELLING THEM IT WASN'T

safe, and that their friends were beyond help. Eventually she resorted to flat-out begging them to return to her home where they could hide out in her warm cellar.

"We'll be back at the spot we left them at any minute, Emily," said Tom. "Please just be quiet until then."

"I hope you don't speak to your mother with such rudeness," she replied, but did him the favour of shutting up afterwards.

Sophie had barely spoken at all since leaving the house, and Tom could see she was lost in her own thoughts. "You okay?" he asked her.

"I think we might be dead."

"What!"

"I was joking before about dying in the crash, but I think it might be true. This isn't a real place, Tom. We have to face facts. I think we died."

"I don't feel dead."

"Me either," she admitted. "I feel normal—at least physically—but this riverbed is unnatural, and..." she leaned in and whispered, "Emily is from the past."

Tom laughed. "Because she doesn't have an iPhone? We're not dead, Soph, but I agree something's going on. I don't believe in ghosts, and neither do you, but perhaps we should consider the possibility."

"You think Emily is a ghost?"

Tom looked back at the odd woman and shrugged. "The hardest part about all this is that I don't know a thing. I have no answers, only a hundred questions. I think we should just agree that whatever is going on, it's not right, and it's not good."

Soph gave him a weak, teary smile. "I'm scared, Tom."

He put an arm around her for the first time in months. "Me too, sweetheart. Me too."

They walked a little longer and Soph spotted movement ahead. "I think that's Patrick."

"There are bones everywhere beneath our feet," Emily warned. "We must go before it's too late."

Soph waved her arms and shouted. "Patrick!"

After the third shout of his name, Patrick stopped whatever he was doing and waved back at them. He looked glad to see them.

They hurried to reach him, and as they got closer, Tom saw Brandon still lying in the mud, propped up on his elbows. He also saw a third person, someone fighting with Patrick.

"He's in trouble!" Tom broke into a sprint, wishing he could run as fast as he could ten years ago. The sinking mud sucked the energy out of him rapidly, and by the time he reached Patrick, he was panting.

Patrick tussled with a young girl covered in mud. He appealed to Tom. "Sodding help me!"

Tom grabbed one of the girl's arms and twisted it behind her back. She didn't cry out in pain, but instead moaned like she was having an orgasm. Stitches kept her mouth from opening.

"No," said Patrick, shaking his head. "Help me calm her down. She's hurt."

"Oh!" Tom let go of the girl's arm and grabbed her legs while Patrick wrapped his arms around her middle. Together, they lowered her down, and Patrick whispered something in the girl's ear. It sounded like he was humming—'Mary had a little lamb,' maybe? Whatever it was, it seemed to work, because the girl's legs stopped kicking, and Tom was able to let go of her.

"Who is she?" Soph asked, catching up to them.

Patrick stopped his humming, but kept a hold of the girl while he answered Sophie. "I don't know. She climbed out of the ground."

Sophie pulled a face. "The ground?"

In the background, Emily clutched her dress and moaned. "The blind monk took her. The silt is his domain. Bones rise in his presence. Blood flows downwards."

Patrick nodded at Emily with a disapproving look on his face. "Who is she?"

"I am Emily Tanner, and you can address me directly."

Patrick kept his attention on Tom. "Is she nuts?"

"What on earth does that mean?" Emily demanded.

"She's..." Tom tried to think of the right word. "Traditional."

"Has she come to help?" Brandon called in a barely decipherable mumble.

Tom shook his head, then remembered he had the broom.

"Not exactly. We can get your leg splinted though. Then maybe we can move you away from here. How you doing?"

"Not good."

"He chewed his tongue," said Patrick. "This is Stacey. Something's been done to her mouth."

Tom stared at the stitches binding the girl's mouth. "Who did that to her?"

Patrick shrugged.

"We need to help her," said Sophie. "Does anybody have anything we can use to cut those stitches?"

Emily stood over the girl. "I shall be able to help her at my house. We must take her there."

Patrick held the girl in his arms and looked at Emily suspiciously. "Your house?"

"Long story," said Tom. "Let's just get Brandon's leg splinted and go."

"No," said Emily. "There is no time for that. Your friends are lucky to still be alive. Let's not tempt fate further."

"What is this bird on about?" said Patrick, looking like he was ready to get up and punch her.

Tom hurried over to Brandon with the broom. "We're not going anywhere until we see to Brandon."

Emily put her palms over her eyes and shook her head. "The bones. They are everywhere. We do not have much time."

"It won't take a minute. Brandon, you okay for me to do this?"

The kid nodded. "Whatever gets me off my ass, man."

Tom got to work. The broom was too long, so he placed it at an angle and stamped on it. Then he took off his belt. The leather was too thick to tear, so he had to ask Patrick to lend his too. He fastened the broom handle against Brandon's shin with both belts, but he still needed to pull it tight. "This will hurt, Brandon. You ready?"

Brandon reached up and shoved his sleeve into his mouth. Then he gave the nod.

"Okay, after three. One.. Two..." Tom yanked the first belt before he got to three. Brandon bellowed and bit down on his sleeve. "Sorry! Okay, last one. After three. One... Two... Three!" This time the scream was not as loud. Patrick watched the whole thing anxiously from nearby. He still had to hold the girl to keep her calm.

Soph put her hand on Tom's back while he knelt in the mud. "Well done."

He tried to keep his focus on Brandon who was fighting back tears and chewing his sleeve. "Okay, Brandon. You did good. If it were me, I'd be bawling my eyes out right now. We'll give you a few minutes to recover and then see if we can get you upright."

"We have no time," Emily kept saying. "He is coming. Look!" She picked up handfuls of bones and let them spill through her hands. "The bones of parishioners, the monk's victims, his minions. He drags them behind him, cursed to forever look upon their remains."

Brandon's eyes rolled around in his head as he fought with consciousness. When he heard Emily's words, it seemed to jolt him awake. "What is she...?"

"Yeah," said Patrick. "What has she been taking? Why did you bring her back with you, Tom? Where's help?"

"There isn't any," said Sophie. "The only thing we found was Emily's house beneath the bridge where we crashed."

Patrick's face lit up. "You found the bridge? What about my truck?"

Tom shook his head.

"I must leave," said Emily, dancing on the spot and fidgeting with her dress. "We are in terrible danger."

"Shut up!" Patrick shouted at her. He covered Stacey's ears to keep from startling her. "Just shut up!"

Emily jolted at the sudden outburst directed at her. "Stay here and face your own ends then, but I am leaving."

"And don't come back," said Patrick petulantly.

Tom sighed. "Patrick, that's not helping. Emily, please don't go rushing off."

Emily had already begun her retreat, but now she stopped in the mud and froze stiff, staring right ahead. She began to mutter something, her voice gaining volume with every word. "No! No! No! NO!"

Tom hurried up to her. "What? What is it?"

"It's too late," she said. "He is here."

In the distance, drawing closer, was a man. He wore a cassock of bleeding flesh and dragged dismembered limbs behind him on chains. His eyes were missing, replaced by jutting silver crucifixes rammed deep into his skull.

"The blind monk," said Tom, unable to take his eyes away. "He's real."

"More real than anything else on this earth," said Emily. "You must run. Now!"

The blind monk stalked the riverbed, bloody chains rattling in his wake.

CHAPTER 8

Emily shoved Tom aside and stood in the path of the abomination. The monk did not increase its speed or show any urgency at all. It shambled.

"You will not harm these people!" Emily shouted.

Tom grabbed her. "Emily, get away!"

But she would not be moved. She glared at Tom and pointed down the riverbed. "You need to leave right now. Trust me! Go to my house and take shelter in the cellar. I shall rejoin you if I can."

Tom grimaced. "If?"

"Go!"

Sophie appeared next to Tom and tugged on him. "Come on! Let's go!"

Brandon was screaming in terror and so was Patrick. Tom wondered why he wasn't doing the same himself and decided it was shock. Must be. He stared at the blind monk in horrified awe—something so vile surely could not be real. It was pain personified, cloaked in flesh, and a length of entrails encircled its throat like a sadistic choker.

Had Sophie been right? Were they dead? Was this Hell?

The Devil shambled toward them.

Patrick cried out for help, trying to drag Brandon to his feet. The young girl, Stacey, snapped out of her stupor and tried to help, but Brandon was a dead weight between them. They couldn't get him up. Sophie kept trying to drag Tom away, but he shrugged free of her and ran to help the others. Between them, they got Brandon upright and hopping on one leg.

"Get me out of here, Dad!" he cried. "Fuck me! What is that thing?"

"I don't know," said Tom, "but you best hop as fast as you can."

Patrick made eye-contact with Tom and nodded a silent thank you for coming back to help. Sophie had made a run for it on her own, but she at least turned back now to wait for them.

They left Emily behind, the small woman standing her ground against a beast twice her height. The monk continued towards her, flesh-coated chains rattling tunefully.

Tom didn't look back again, and neither did anybody else. They carried Brandon between them and got the hell out of there. Eventually, they were far enough from danger to slow down, but Emily's defiant shouts still echoed in the distance behind them. "It's me you want, Father! Come and get me."

"We can't just leave her," Tom said, ashamed of himself for waiting until he was this far away to say it.

"Screw her," said Sophie. "This is her deal, not ours. She and that... that *thing* obviously have history—let's not get in the middle of it."

Tom didn't like it, but he nodded anyway. Even if he wanted to go back, the monster terrified him.

Patrick was huffing and puffing. "She told us to go to her house. Where is it?"

"Downriver," said Tom. "It's still a way to go."

Brandon groaned. Sweat poured from his forehead as he hopped again and again. Each time he landed, it shook his dangling broken leg and made him groan. "I don't think I can go on much longer. It hurts too much."

"Just lean on me, son," said Patrick, giving off a fair amount of sweat himself.

"I can't, Dad. You're about to keel over too."

Tom agreed. Patrick was bright red and wheezing. "How do you cope as a builder?"

"By telling labourers what to do," he shot back, visibly annoyed.

Brandon stopped his hopping and looked at his dad. "No, you're not usually like this. You eat and drink like a pig, but I've seen you shovel cement for six hours straight. What's wrong with you?"

Patrick let go of his son and put his hands on his hips while he caught his breath. Stacey stood beside him, concerned. It was obvious she felt safest next to Patrick because of him taking care of her earlier.

"I dunno," he admitted. "Just finding it hard to catch my wind. Started a little while back when we tried to climb the banks."

"That's when my throat started hurting," said Sophie, giving her neck a quick squeeze.

"We don't have time for this," said Tom. In the corner of his eye, he saw bones rising from the ground. "We have to get to Emily's house."

"I can't make it," said Brandon, wobbling on one leg. "I need to take a break."

Tom sighed and fought to keep the lad from tipping over. "You stay here and that-that... FUCK!" He felt like he was losing his mind. "I don't know what the hell that thing is, but I know it'll rip our insides out if it gets anywhere near us."

"The blind monk," said Sophie. "Emily was telling the truth."

"What the hell are you talking about?" Patrick demanded. "What the hell is happening?"

"We're dead," said Sophie matter-of-factly.

Tom told her she was wrong. She had to be. "If we're dead, then why would you have a sore throat? Do you think people get the sniffles in Hell? Ebola would be more the Devil's style, surely?"

Sophie rubbed her throat again and seemed to consider it. "Whatever this place is, we're somewhere bad."

More bones oozed from the ground. Everyone noticed, but nobody mentioned it. A breeze blew along the riverbed, gathering bluster. Thunder clashed, closer than ever. Tom turned a full circle. "Sophie's right. Something's wrong here."

"No shit," said Brandon.

"No," he said, "something bad's happening right now."

The breeze became a gale.

The riverbed shifted.

Thunder clashed a second time.

Sophie screamed. A hand burst forth from the mud and seized her by the ankle. Tom kicked out at a blackened claw rising beside his foot while another came up behind him and grabbed his calf. Sophie stumbled onto her knees and a hand burst forth and grabbed her wrist. "Tom! Help me!"

Nearby, Stacey moaned through her stitches and leapt about. A dozen grasping hands surrounded the girl, and she danced between them. Brandon bellowed as a hand wrapped around his broken shin. Patrick saw his son's peril and threw himself down in the mud, but before he could do anything, he found himself seized by half a dozen hands bursting forth from the ground.

Tom hurried over to Sophie and yanked her back to her feet just as a hand attempted to rake her face. She was stark white, and looked at Tom through misty, traumatised eyes. "Tom! Tom, I'm sorry. I'm sorry I cheated on you. I'm sorry I made you unhappy. Just make this all stop. Please!"

"Don't!" he shouted, stamping on a hand grasping for his foot and breaking its fingers. "It doesn't matter. We need to get out of here."

"We can't!"

"Help my boy!" Patrick shouted to them desperately. Countless hands were yanking him down into the mud. "Help Brandon!"

The wind increased. Tom had to shield his face as he searched for the kid. He spotted him on the ground, ten feet away. He was clutching his ruined leg and trying to fight off attacks from all sides. It was a losing battle.

Tom didn't know who needed his help more.

Stacey moaned and stared at him pleadingly.

Sophie stood frozen in shock.

Brandon screamed in pain.

Patrick bellowed. Tom turned just in time to see the builder's chunky arm snap back at the elbow. He was half sunken in the mud by now, body tilting downwards like the Titanic slipping beneath the waves. He blew air from his cheeks as he fought with all he had, and as he locked eyes with Tom, right at the end, he mouthed a final message. "Help my boy."

Tom nodded.

He sprang into action, cutting a path to Brandon. "Help me," the lad wailed, even though that's exactly what Tom was trying to do.

"Get up, kid! Help me get you out of here."

Brandon clutched at Tom, his grasping hands like the ones bursting forth from the earth. His right leg was useless, but sheer terror helped him fight his way onto his left side. Tom wrapped an arm around him and dragged him out of there. The wind was so harsh that dust and bone fragments hit their skin and blinded them. Roving hands grabbed at their ankles ceaselessly, yet somehow they made it back to Sophie. Stacey was already there, and the three of them carried Brandon between them.

"You were right!" Tom grabbed Sophie by the shoulders and looked her in the face. "We are dead."

"No, you are not," came a rasping voice. "At least, not yet." A cloaked figure rushed towards them so fast he could have struck them down dead before they could even cry out. But the stranger did not strike them. Instead, he drew a sword from inside a thick black cloak and wielded it like a samurai. He swiped at the ground and sent fingers and knuckle-bones scattering into the wind.

"Who are you?" Tom demanded, yet knew enough that he was glad to meet this stranger.

"Come on!" The swordsman sliced through another crop of grasping hands. "We must go to the house."

Tom shook his head. "What house?"

"The house beneath the bridge."

The sound of rattling chains echoed off the riverbanks.

☙❧

THEY FOLLOWED THE STRANGER IN SILENCE. HE HAD TAKEN charge so forcefully that no one dared speak, and they fought against the billowing wind until they simply stepped out of it. Once again, they were walking through the wet mud of the empty riverbed. Brandon hopped between Tom and Sophie while Stacey wandered slightly behind.

They saw the bridge.

"It's changed," Tom muttered. "It's not as high, or as big. It's different."

"No," said the stranger. "It is only we who change. What is down here is not what is above."

Sophie glanced at Tom wearily. Would things ever make sense again? God, how he was hankering for a spreadsheet and Monday morning coffee.

"Who are you?" Tom asked again. "What are those shapes moving up on the bridge?"

The stranger turned around. A hood obscured his face, but two small, serious eyes looked out at them. "Let us reach safety. Then we shall talk."

Sophie laughed. Tom frowned. "You think something's funny?"

"Funny, absurd, soul-destroying, whatever. I'm just having the worst day ever."

Tom felt the weight of Brandon leaning on his shoulder and glanced at Stacey with her lips stitched shut. "I think we're all having a bad day, Soph."

She didn't disagree. In fact, she nodded. "I suppose I'm just wanting to know when this ends. In which scenario do you see us climbing out of this riverbed and going back to civilisation? People don't experience stuff like this and go on to tell their local newspaper about it afterwards. Fuck! I always promised myself I wouldn't die in this goddamn place."

"We're not dead yet. Captain Wow told us so."

She chuckled. "Till Death Do Us Part. I suppose you and I will be together until the end after all."

"Soph!"

"Sorry. I just... When those hands were grabbing me, I was so scared. I thought I was going to die. You came to help me, and I loved you again for a minute. I wanted to wrap my arms around you and hold you forever. You were my hero, my soulmate."

"And now?"

"Now I realise it was adrenaline. We're back to walking along this riverbed with no clue what's going on. I think about how much easier it would've been if those hands had pulled me beneath the ground and killed me like Patrick. Maybe it's what I deserve."

While he could not let go of Brandon, he managed to reach around the kid's back and grab Sophie's hand. "Stop blaming yourself."

"*You* blame me."

"Yes," he admitted. "I blame you for cheating on me instead of having the guts to just end it. You slept with our neighbour, Soph! I mean... fuck! I blame you for that, hell yes—you suck—but I don't hate you, and I don't want to see you suffer. I know you wouldn't have set out to hurt me. Time to move on, just like you've been saying these last few weeks. I'm on your side, even when I'm not."

"I'm sorry I cheated on you, Tom—but that's not what I'm talking about. You blame me for not having children."

He almost dropped Brandon then, who was in so much pain that he paid little attention to what was being said. The kid had also just lost his father and so had bigger things to mourn than Tom and Sophie's marriage.

Tom grunted. "That's not true, Soph. How can I blame you for something that's not your fault? You can't help it that you can't conceive."

"You might not blame me rationally, but deep down you wonder what you did to deserve a barren wife. The more years have passed, the angrier you've become. I see it every time you look at me. Can you honestly say it doesn't bother you?"

Tom readjusted his grip on Brandon. "It does bother me, Soph. Of course it does. I always wanted kids. You did too. That's why I couldn't understand why we stopped with the IVF."

"Because it wasn't working. Each time it failed you got angrier about all the money wasted. It was like you thought I was doing it on purpose. You cancelled our holiday to Cyprus after the last time, said we couldn't afford it, but I knew you were doing it out of spite. You didn't want to be around me, or see me having fun. I didn't deserve it."

"I..." He wanted to tell her how stupid she was being, but maybe she was right. He had made her feel this way whether it had been intentional or not. He couldn't tell her she didn't feel how she did. "I should've been a better husband. I focused so hard on having the perfect life that I ruined the one I had. Soph, I'm so sorry."

"All I ever wanted was you, Tom. I wanted a husband who was around instead of at work all the time. A husband who would cry with me each time the IVF failed instead of getting frustrated and mean. I may have cheated on you, Tom, but you left me years ago."

His eyes filled with tears, so he looked up to keep them from spilling down his cheeks. They had now passed directly beneath the bridge, and he could see the crumbling mortar between the ancient stones and the fading graffiti of past youth. It was too high to reach, but much closer than before.

"The house," said the stranger. "It is here."

This was not the house Tom had seen before. This one was much larger and made from logs not stone. The roof was formed of heavy timbers. "What is this? The house we saw earlier was different."

The stranger unfastened his coat in preparation of going inside. "The house beneath the bridge is never the same twice, but it is always safe. There are many of us assembled here, so the house is bigger to accommodate. Come inside, friends."

Glad to be off the riverbed and away from its horrors, they willingly obliged, stepping through the narrow front door one by one. Inside was warm and dry, with stout floorboards and thick timber walls. There was no electricity, but the interior was lit by weak light shining through the windows.

Five chairs lay in a semi-circle, one for each of them, and Tom helped Brandon sit down on the nearest before collapsing into the next. Sophie was about to take a seat, too, but Stacey grabbed her. The girl pointed to her mouth.

Sophie nodded with understanding. "Oh shit, yes. We need to cut Stacey's stitches." She turned to the stranger. "Can you help her, please?"

"It shall be my pleasure." The stranger removed his hood, revealing a mildly handsome man with shoulder length brown hair in need of a wash. He reached inside his cloak and pulled out a small, homemade blade—handle wrapped in twine. He approached Stacey with it a little too hastily and the girl cowered.

Sophie took her arm. "It's okay. You're safe."

The stranger smiled reassuringly and raised the knife to Stacey's face. "This might be uncomfortable, miss, for it shall tug at your wounds."

Stacey groaned, and her eyes rolled, but she gave the nod. The stranger pressed his knife against the first stitch on the right and began to saw away. Stacey whimpered. Tom winced at the sight of her bloody wounds stretching. Who had done such a thing to her? The blind monk?

"Who are you?" Sophie asked the stranger as he worked.

Finally, he gave an answer. "My name is Jonathan Tanner. I am —I was—a lowly tailor in Abbeydale. Now I am just one of its few remaining residents. My wife, Emily, and I."

"Emily?" Tom enquired. "You live here together?"

"No, we are separated—by many things. I betrayed her."

Tom knew what that felt like. Sophie folded her arms and looked away in what he assumed was shame.

"How did you betray her?" asked Brandon, looking grim as he avoided looking at both Stacey's stitches and his own ruined leg.

Jonathan started on another stitch, making Stacey flinch. "There was a witch in Abbeydale. We had known it for a while. Livestock would grow sickly and die, people's skin would fester and boil. Milk left beyond a day would sour. All signs of a vileness in our midst. Then, one day, the murders began. The first child found was Annabel Stone. Someone had dragged her out of her bed in the small hours and weighted her down with rocks in the shallow stream nearby. She had drowned slowly, catching a breath now and then whenever the river ebbed. The dead toad stuffed in her mouth told us what we were dealing with. The toad is a foul creature that only a Hell-whore would worship."

Tom frowned. "Okay..."

Jonathan cut another stitch and Stacey's legs trembled. Tom considered that they should be doing this sitting down.

Jonathan, however, continued his tale standing. "Several more children were murdered over the next three years, until people in the village stopped trying to conceive for fear of their own spawn being taken. Father Cotton would visit from the abbey often, to warn us that the Devil was feeding off our sin and thriving among us, but we were all good people. Great evil has no motive but wickedness itself. The Devil's servant revealed itself as my wife."

"Emily?" said Tom. "Emily is a witch?"

Jonathan nodded gravely. "The village school teacher, Martha Hamleigh, found her twin girls missing one night and knew right away that the witch had taken them. She set out into the night, heading for the stream where we had first found Annabel Stone. There she found her children dead, and Emily stuffing toads into their mouths. She did this whilst completely naked, adding further indecency to the act."

"Holy shit," said Brandon.

"But it was all fallacy," said Jonathan, lowering his knife for a moment and staring into space. "Martha was the true witch, drowning her own children once they came of age. We did not know the truth of it then, though, and even I believed her wretched tale as she spoke it in the village square. I condemned my dear Emily right alongside everybody else." He stopped for a moment and stared at his hands. "We burnt her at the stake."

"What?" Sophie was shaking her head. "This is all a bunch of nonsense, surely? There's no such thing as witches, and we don't burn people at the stake, not even in this backwards village. I should know, I lived here long enough."

"You are from the village?" asked Jonathan. "Interesting. Well, I assure you, good lady, that there is very much such a thing as witches, and we do indeed burn them at the stake. It is the only way to save what remains of their soul."

Brandon rubbed a spot of blood from his chin and grunted. "You're off your head, mate. It's 2017, not—"

"It was 1626 when we put Emily to death," said Jonathan, turning from Stacey and facing the chairs. "You are not the first to fall upon our damnation since then, but you are the latest. It has been a long time, perhaps a hundred years, since I spoke to another person like this, and those poor souls barely knew the history of this place at all. They spoke of wars and great strife. It is good to know the world did not end then."

Sophie cackled, and Tom wondered if she was losing a grip. She took a deep breath and said, "One hundred years? We're supposed to believe you've been alive for centuries? How is that possible?"

Jonathan smiled, but it was a weary, tired expression that suggested he might well have been around for a hundred years. "I shall never leave this place. I shall never grow old or enjoy the respite of death. Martha will not allow it. We all must suffer. You see, once we burned Emily, Martha gleefully revealed herself. Our shared sin of burning an innocent woman damned us all. We gave the Devil the power to punish us, and Martha was his instrument to do so. She cursed Father Cotton first, for he had been the ring-leader of Emily's persecution. His punishment: to walk the riverbed cloaked in the flesh of his flock, bones and blood of his parishioners forever rising in his wake. I, and the rest of the villagers, were damned to an eternity in this empty riverbed, and me never to be reunited with my dear Emily, denied any chance of atoning for my betrayal. Of all the souls in Cottontree, only Emily could ascend to Heaven—the only among us who was innocent. I hope she is at peace."

"Emily's not in Heaven," said Tom. "She's here. She helped us escape the blind monk."

Jonathan started and turned pale. He moved away from Stacey and stared at Tom. "W-what you say cannot be true. Emily is inno-cent. Why would she be damned? Why would she walk the silt with the rest of us? This cannot be right."

"I don't know what to tell you," said Tom. "She said her name was Emily. We met her at this house—a different house."

Jonathan nodded. "She is here then... damned like the rest of us. My dear Emily. Has she not suffered enough? She must have been here the whole time, but my curse... it prevents me from ever seeing her."

Tom and Sophie looked at each other awkwardly.

"This is my chance to make things right," said Jonathan. "My chance to reach her and save her soul."

"But you're cursed to forever be apart," said Brandon, listing in his chair and threatening to fall off.

"My spirit and Emily's may never come together, but you fine people can help me. You fine people can tell her how sorry I am, and that I will do all I can to end her suffering. Perhaps she has remained here this whole time awaiting such a promise. You shall help me, yes?"

There was a gagging noise at the edge of the room. They hadn't realised it, but Stacey had been pulling at her remaining stitches while they'd been talking. Tom felt bad for forgetting about her. She stepped into the centre of the room and pulled a long bloody thread from a large hole in her upper lip. The final stitch. Then she doubled over and wretched.

A dead toad splatted on the floorboards.

She followed it up with watery puke.

CHAPTER 9

Patrick awoke with a scream. Hands all over his body, clutching him, pulling him, suffocating him. He was dead. Hell had dragged him beneath the earth and into damnation. How much punishment had he earned during his mortal life? Had he been a bad man? Surely not? In the grand scheme of things, he had lived a mundane and uneventful life. Not the best of husbands, perhaps, but he didn't beat his wife or cheat on her all the time. Nor had he ever struck Brandon—except for on that one single occasion, and that had been a moment of madness. He'd always been there for his boy. He'd been there for Brandon after other fathers would have slung their hooks. Perhaps that was the specific reason he was damned. Covering his son's sins had made them his own.

I do deserve to be here then. I'm in Hell.

He got up off the floor, joints clicking, and looked around. He remembered his arm snapping back at the elbow, but now it was fine. As far as Hell went, it was bland. The floor was stone, and the walls rose up on either side to meet in an apex, forming some kind of chamber. At the end of the chamber was a set of stone steps, beyond which lay a church.

What is a church doing in Hell?

It was an austere structure with a simple spire at the front. The back of the building branched left and right but only by a few feet.

What Patrick knew about churches he could write on the back of a stamp, so he could describe nothing other than it was made of stone and it was old. There were no windows or openings anywhere aside from a small space at the front where one could enter. Last thing he planned on doing, though, was going inside. Whatever was in that church, it wouldn't be good.

Perhaps this was one of Hell's games—offer the salvation of a church, only to fill it with unbearable horrors. Did demons dwell inside? Would they spill out and chase him through the chamber he now found himself in? Where did the chamber lead in the other direction? Only one way to find out.

Patrick started walking and whistled for no other reason than it felt good to break the silence. He felt somewhat defiant too. Sure, he had been no great man, but he'd done nothing to truly hurt anyone either. Racist chats down the pub weren't the same as fire-bombing a mosque. His sexist views were a facet of his generation and something he had been ingrained with long before he ever gave politics any real consideration. No, he wasn't a saint, but he didn't deserve to be here—not Hell. It wasn't right that he was dead.

That it resulted from a car crash made things even worse.

They'd be chatting about his death down the Hog's Head tonight, along with the rest of the other local gossip. Why couldn't he have had a heart attack at sixty like his old man? That was the man's way to go, before any of the weakness of old age set in. Go out like a man while you were still a man. Instead, he had gone off the side of a bloody bridge and drowned in the river. And since then things had only got nastier.

That sick fuck with the chains. The hands dragging him into the earth. It should have been obvious from the start that none of them had walked away from the crash in one piece. Tom, Sophie, him, and...

God, Brandon. My son is dead too.

They had woken up on the riverbed together. A broken leg was just the first of Bran's many torments. There would be more. For both of them. This was Hell after all.

Patrick glanced back at that church to see if anything had spilled out of the entrance to follow him. Nothing had, but that didn't mean there was no cause for concern. He'd been walking away from the small chapel, but somehow, impossibly, as he looked back now, he had got closer to it. His journey forward had taken him backwards.

"Fuck this!" He ran—only at a jog for he was too ample to manage more, but just as on the riverbed, he found himself short of breath. This time, he refused to succumb to it. If this was Hell, then perhaps his fitness levels were all in his mind. You had to be alive to be winded, surely? You didn't need to breathe when you were dead.

"Just keep going!" he told himself. "Just... keep... going."

But it was useless. After a few minutes, he was done for. He stopped running and doubled over in agony, panting and gasping for breath. It felt like he might die a second time, from that heart attack he had wished for. Although he dreaded what he might see, he turned back to face the church again. The stone steps were now at his toes. The steeple's shadow fell over him.

"Fuck you!" he shouted, then turned again to run, determined to win this war.

A ruined face—eyes obliterated by silver crucifixes—stared back at him. Chains rattled. The blind monk reached out to Patrick, twisted fingers dripping flesh from weeping nail beds. Patrick screamed and ducked just in time to avoid being grabbed. The creature moved slowly, which was a good thing as Patrick stumbled backwards onto the church steps. His back struck the harsh stone, and he roared in pain, but he was too terrified to care. He crawled backwards like a spider, screaming the entire time. The stench of death washed over him. The reek of damnation.

Now, the church Patrick had sought to avoid became his only sanctuary. He scrambled to his feet at the top of the steps and clambered through the small opening into the church.

Behind him, the monster rattled its chains.

Two rows of long wooden pews filled the bulk of the church's interior with a space between leading to an elevated altar at the front. There was a wide space behind the altar with more benches and a table draped in cloth and adorned with candles. Although the church outside had possessed no windows, its interior was illuminated via floor to ceiling stained glass windows, each one depicting scenes Patrick imagined were from the bible.

Two girls sat in the pews, looking back at him curiously.

The rattle of chains still in his ears, Patrick glanced back, expecting to see the monk shambling through the opening after him, but instead he saw a pair of thick wooden doors.

The two girls looked concerned, but they didn't try to run or scream. "I'm not dangerous," he assured them. "My name is Patrick. I was in a car crash. Am I... is this Hell?"

Of the two girls, one was coffee-skinned with waist-length brown hair. The other was a slender white girl with reddish-gold hair and was a looker. "We don't know where we are," she said, "but this place is safe. Father Cotton has been looking after us."

Patrick studied the empty church. "Father Cotton? Where is he?"

The wooden doors behind Patrick flew open and the blind monk appeared. He wheeled backwards down the aisle, heart in his chest. The safety of the church had been an illusion, and now he was trapped with no place to go. The girls in the pews were saying something, but he could not understand. His focus was solely on the vile creature shambling through the doors.

The beast passed into the church and placed a mangled foot into a shaft of light spilling through one of the stained-glass windows.

It changed.

The monster stepped into the light and became a man. Whatever parts remained in shadow were still horrid—bleeding, festering flesh—but within the light the beast was just a man. A priest in fact. He wore the drab robes of a monk.

The monk smiled at Patrick as he fully entered the light of the aisle. He made no threatening moves or overtures of any kind, and everything about him seemed gentle. "Welcome to my church," he said. "I am Father Cotton."

Patrick swallowed razer blades, and for a moment, he thought he might faint. The two girls appeared just in time to catch him and guide him onto a pew. The girl with the reddish-blonde hair sat beside him and rubbed his back. "Father Cotton is okay. You're safe now."

"At least within these four walls," the priest added. "I am afraid my protection does not extend further. Before the village was cast into damnation, the monks at the abbey had time to pray. This church was the answer they received."

"My name is Mia," said the dark girl, still standing, "and this is Gwen."

"Nice to meet you, Patrick," said Gwen, still rubbing his back. "I think we crashed into each other."

Patrick's eyes widened. "You're the girls from the other car?"

Gwen nodded. "We woke up in the mud a few days ago. Couldn't find our car or the bridge or anyone to help us. We walked for days until we found a little cottage with a woman inside."

Patrick glanced at the priest, to make sure he wasn't about to turn back into a monster and attack him, but the man stood with his hands clasped calmly, so he turned back to Gwen. "Tom and Sophie said the same thing. They came back from some house with a woman named Emily."

"The woman you met is not Emily Tanner," said Father Cotton. "Her name is Martha Hamleigh, and she is a witch. She uses Emily's name just to spite me—to rub my nose in my biggest sin."

Every time Patrick thought the rabbit hole might end, it only got wider and deeper. "Witches, monks, Hell, Heaven... whatever this ride is, I'm ready to get off. I mean, Jesus fucking Christ!" He glanced at Father Cotton. "Sorry, Father."

The priest smiled. "There are worse things than swearing, my child. Do not fret."

"Where is this place?" He looked at Gwen again. "You said you woke up a few days ago? That's not possible. I was in a car crash today, I'm sure of it. Are you saying I was unconscious for three days?"

"Time does not exist here," said Father Cotton. "At least not in relation to itself."

Patrick groaned. Any more of this and his mind would shatter. "Am I dead?"

"Possibly," said Father Cotton. "Near, at the very least."

"What does that mean?"

"The bridge you crossed is cursed. The people of Abbeydale used to hang people from it, and we burned a witch alive beneath the ancient oak tree leaning beside it. That oak tree eventually fell into the river and took the village's sins with it. Beneath the bridge is a place of damnation, and you fell upon it mortally wounded. Your blood is like honey to the forces of darkness. Your trauma brought you here and cast you into our damnation. It is only supposed to be the villagers of Abbeydale who dwell here. I am sorry for your misfortune."

"I don't believe in witches," said Patrick.

"Then what do you believe in?"

"What I can see with my own two eyes."

Father Cotton smiled warmly. "And what have they shown you?"

It was a good point, and not one Patrick could argue against. "What are you? Outside the church, you were a monster. Tom called you the blind monk."

"And that is what I am and forever damned to be."

"Why?"

"Because I was a holy man who led his flock to damnation. It was my fervour that saw a great misdeed take place, and it is I who deserve eternal punishment more than any other. Outside of this church, I am an abomination, the kind of monstrosity I was compelled to find and punish when I was alive. I was a poor servant of God, Patrick—self-righteous and fundamental in my beliefs. I saw wickedness where there was none, and saw monsters where there were only flawed and decent human beings. Now, I am the monster that corrupts, and I drag behind me the flesh of the innocent souls I failed to save. I am truly damned."

"But you're not evil?"

The question made the priest close his eyes. "I don't know what I am anymore. My notions of God, of good and evil, have all faded with time. All I can say is that I am uninterested in seeing anyone join me in my agonising afterlife. I would see you all return to the lives you may still lead."

Patrick's lips were dry, so he licked them. It was hard to speak. "There's a way out of this place?"

"Possibly."

"How?"

"By ending the corruption that keeps you here. We must put an end to the mocking whore presenting herself as Emily Tanner. And the man who aids her, Emily's former husband, Jonathan."

"Who's Jonathan?"

Father Cotton shuddered. "A man far worse than any witch."

◈✦◈

"HERE, MISS, DRINK THIS." JONATHAN HANDED STACEY A PEWTER mug filled with water. "The river might be dry, but the house still provides everything one needs."

"What do you mean?" asked Sophie.

As Stacey sipped at her water and tried to keep from vomiting again, Jonathan stepped into the corner of the room. Tom and Sophie followed him instinctively. "This house," he said in a whisper, "was built by God."

Sophie smirked. Neither she nor Tom had much time for religion, but she held more contempt for it than he did. She looked around now with a scornful eyebrow raised. "God built this place? Can't say I love his taste."

Jonathan frowned. "Its appearance is unimportant, a mere reflection of those who enter. What is important is that this house is a sanctuary. What dwells without cannot come within. The cellar is stocked with supplies. You shall be safe there."

"But not if we leave?" asked Tom, trying to understand things. He was failing to see how staying in this odd house helped the situation.

Jonathan saw the consternation on his face and addressed him. "Do you doubt the sanctity of this place, brother?"

"No. No, I believe you. I just... don't think we're any better off being stuck here."

Jonathan sighed. "I am sorry that you are here, but it is the only place you may be safe. When Martha cursed the village, the monks at the abbey made one last plea for mercy from God. They asked Him to protect Abbeydale from evil. This house was God's reply."

"You think he might have done more," Emily quipped, her arms now folded as she visibly lost patience.

"Darkness is not without might," said Jonathan. "It would not exist otherwise. I imagine the Lord did all He could."

Tom didn't want to offend the man, but he couldn't get

onboard with the God-talk. "How do we leave this place? How do we get back to where we came from?"

Jonathan looked at him. "There is no way, brother. No one leaves the riverbed. We are all here forever—snared by the most powerful of spells."

Tom saw Sophie clench her fists. He reached out subtly and squeezed her arm—there was no point getting angry. To Jonathan he said, "I don't believe what you say. We got here somehow, and that means we can get out."

"Foolish logic, brother. You cannot leave, but I believe you are here for a reason. I need to reach my Emily. She deserves peace."

"So do we," said Tom. "We're not interested in helping you if you won't help us."

Jonathan breathed heavily, like he was trying to contain an unbridled rage. Tom eyed the sword on the man's belt and wondered how deep his delusions ran.

"Look," said Sophie. "We don't belong here. We didn't burn any witches. None of what happened here is our fault. You might deserve damnation, but we don't. At least, we don't deserve *your* damnation. I've got sins of my own to answer for, thank you very much."

Jonathan sighed. "Okay. Fine, I shall try to help you, if only to show you the futility of the situation. Nobody has ever escaped this place, but perhaps there is yet a way."

"What?" asked Tom eagerly.

"You must kill the blind monk. He is the totem that centres this place. Martha channelled all of her wickedness into the loathsome creature to act as her guardian and servant. To extinguish him would be to extinguish Martha's spell. Then, you might be able to leave. Perhaps we could all move on."

"Why haven't you killed the blind monk yourself?"

"I have hidden in the riverbed for hundreds of years because I felt I deserved my punishment, and that my dear Emily was in a better place. Today, I learned that not to be true. If Emily is here, then I can be a coward no longer. I must face and kill the monk. Help me."

"Us help you?" said Sophie, incredulous.

"We'll help each other," said Tom. "I don't want to face that monster any more than you do, Soph, but a battle with it is inevitable, three and three makes six. We can't stay in this house and do nothing."

"How can we kill something like that, Tom? You won't even kill a spider."

"You should not," said Jonathan curtly. "Spiders control the fly population. Without them, we would be mired in pestilence."

"Exactly!" said Tom.

Sophie bristled. "Can we stick to the issues that matter, please?" She left them standing in the corner and went back to Brandon and Stacey—their pair of young casualties. "How are you both feeling?"

Tom had done his best to splint Brandon's leg, but the kid had a waxy, pale complexion that didn't suggest he was doing well. All the same, he managed a weak smile when Sophie approached him. "The pain is a little better. Only mild agony now. What have you all been talking about?"

"The blind monk," said Soph.

"What is that thing?" asked Stacey, now able to talk. She had the usual, annoying tone of a teenage girl, full of unnecessary emphasis and poor word choice, and she swore a lot. "It looked like the mother fucking Devil."

"He is not the Devil," said Jonathan.

"Was it the monk who stitched shut your mouth?" Sophie asked the girl.

She fingered her swollen lips as if she had forgotten about them for a moment. "I don't know. I woke up covered in mud. Thought I was going to suffocate, but Brandon's dad pulled me out. Yes, though, I think it was the monk."

"Patrick seems to rescue a lot of people," said Tom. "He pulled me out of the mud too."

"I'm the only one who got fucking butchered though," Stacey sulked. "Why did that bastard pick on me? I say we kill that piece of shit."

"Your tongue is most foul," said Jonathan, more curiously than chiding. "You are a girl."

Stacey pulled a face. "So fucking what?"

Jonathan looked at the others. "I understand her injuries now."

"What do you mean?" Tom asked.

"The monk sees our sins and punishes accordingly. This girl is diseased of mouth. Her lips were sewn shut. The monk's work for sure. He needs to be stopped once and for all."

Sophie pointed at the wet mess in the centre of the room. "What about the frog?"

Jonathan walked over to the dead animal and flicked it into the corner with his boot. He remained there, staring at the dark stain it left behind. "Martha's calling card. She exerts control over the blind monk. His actions are her demands. They are as one."

"So, we kill the monk, we hurt the witch," said Sophie, summing things up as she often liked to do.

"Yes!"

"We can't fight that fucking thing," said Tom.

"And I didn't deserve to get my fu—my flipping—mouth sewn shut," said Stacey, getting steamed up.

"Of course you didn't," said Sophie calmly. "But I don't think we should fight that thing either."

"You must," urged Jonathan.

"Yes!" agreed Stacey.

"All I am interested in," Sophie said in a voice that brooked no argument, "is getting out of this place. You burned an innocent woman at the stake, Jonathan, and now you're paying for it. Not my place to question the nature of damnation or whatever it is, but I'll get what's coming to me when it's my time. Until then, you can fight your own battles."

Jonathan tugged at the lapels of his jacket and folded his arms. "That is disappointing."

"Do you have any vodka in this place, dude?" Brandon mumbled. "Something to dull the pain?"

"Yeah," said Stacey, her one eye twitching strangely. "What about WKD?"

Jonathan frowned, and to Tom he said, "I do not understand their words."

"Never mind. Can you help us escape here without us having to face the blind monk?"

Jonathan took a moment to consider. He walked a circle around the room, his boots clicking on the thick floorboards. Then his footsteps echoed hollowly, and he stopped walking. Tom saw the square frame cut into the floorboards and knew what it was. "What's in the cellar, Jonathan?"

"Whatever one needs. The cellar is the house's way of providing. Food, water, tools. You shall find it in the cellar. Without it, eternity here would be unbearable."

Sophie huffed. "It's some kind of magical grotto, is it?"

"It is whatever it needs to be. If you wish to leave, then perhaps the cellar will provide what you require."

Tom stared at the hatch, wondering what good ever came from a trapdoor. "Like what? What could it do to help us?"

Jonathan stepped off the hatch and removed his sword.

Everyone in the room flinched, but he wasn't intending to use it on them. He shoved the point into the gap between the frame and levered the sword until the hatch popped open. Reaching down, he shoved his fingers under the hatch and lifted.

"Only one way to find out," he said with a grin.

The cellar was dark, and only a square of inky blackness greeted them.

"What do we have to lose?" said Sophie, standing up and walking to the edge.

"Exactly," said Stacey. "We need to do whatever it takes to get out of this place. Let's just go down."

"No," said Tom.

Jonathan frowned. "But it is the only way, my friend. If you will not help me vanquish the evil from this place, then you must search for answers elsewhere. The cellar shall guide you."

Sophie looked at Tom, ignoring the others. "What's wrong?"

At first it had been a subtle tingle, like tummy ache, but when Jonathan stood on that trapdoor, it had provoked a full on feeling of déjà vu. Red flags were waving in the back of his mind. "Emily wanted us to go down into the cellar, too."

Jonathan nodded. "Of course. She knows it is safe down there."

"I'm not convinced. Seemed like she was more interested in us going down in the cellar than anything else. Why?"

Jonathan flapped his arms theatrically. "I don't know. It has been an age since I last saw her, but I imagine she wanted to see you safe, as I do."

Tom frowned. "You were eager for us to help you reach Emily when we first mentioned her, but when we refused you switched tactics to us killing the monk. Now you want us to go down to the cellar. It doesn't add up."

Jonathan turned his back and made an audible sound of irritation. "You people do as you please. I am sorry you have been dragged into our affairs, but I cannot force you to do anything. If you will not help me find my Emily, I shall find another way to reach her. If I must face the blind monk alone, I shall. But rest assured, the cellar is your only chance of surviving this damned place. It provides."

"I'm not going down there," said Tom, making his decision final.

"Me either," said Sophie, taking a step back from the edge.

"I don't care, to be honest," said Brandon, blinking slowly. "I'm screwed whatever we do."

"No, you're not!" Sophie snapped back at him. "We will get you help, Brandon, I promise."

"The only help you shall find is in the cellar." Jonathan lifted his sword and pointed it at Sophie's throat. "Now, please, make your way down the ladder. Manipulation is such a meandering way to get things done, so let's make things simpler."

Sophie put her hands up, wincing as the blade scratched her throat.

"What are you doing?" Tom demanded.

"Taking charge of unruly guests. I saved you from a fate worse than death, and you repay me with obstinacy. Down the hatch now, you wretched oafs!"

Sophie tried to sidestep, but Jonathan moved with her. As a reward, he flicked his wrist and drew blood from her cheek. Instead of crying, she snarled.

"Okay," said Tom, hands up where everyone could see them. "I'll go down the hatch."

"Tom! Don't!" Sophie received another slash on her opposite cheek for that, and this time she had to bite her lip to keep from crying out.

"It's okay." Tom edged towards the trapdoor, peering down into the darkness. He could still see nothing, but the first rung of a wooden ladder and he stepped down onto it, but then, instead of descending further, he leapt back out of the hole and tackled Jonathan around the knees. His old rugby days came back to him, and he toppled the swordsman easily.

Sophie shouted out triumphantly. "Punch him in the balls, Tom!"

Jonathan tried to bring up his sword, but at close quarters, he couldn't get it around. Tom punched him in the jaw and grunted with pain as his fist almost broke. He followed up a left hook. Now both hands were aching, so he choked Jonathan.

Jonathan hooted with laughter. Unsettled, Tom removed his hands from the man's throat and asked him, "What are you laughing at?"

"You cannot kill what is already dead." Jonathan grabbed for his sword again, but Tom punched him in the eye.

"You still feel pain though. Sophie, get some rope or something. I want answers."

Sophie nodded and turned to obey, but there was the sound of an almighty blow, and instead, she toppled sideways through the hatch and disappeared from sight.

"Sophie!" Tom reached out to her, but it was too late, and the moment's distraction meant Jonathan reclaimed his sword. The blade moved too quickly, and the fingers of Tom's right hand splayed apart as sharp metal slid through his palm and erupted out the other side. He yelled so hard his throat burned.

Stacey rushed towards Tom, still brandishing the iron poker she'd struck Sophie in the temple with. Jonathan withdrew the sword from his hand and ignited another flourish of pain before shoving him backwards into the hatch.

CHAPTER 10

"Jonathan Tanner was a warlock when he was alive, posing as a simple tailor," said Father Cotton. "It was he who corrupted Martha to the ways of darkness. He who worshipped at the shrine of the Horned Toad—Chordaxis. Martha served his every need, both physically and supernaturally."

Patrick leant forward in the pew and rubbed at his forehead. Gwen obviously saw the weary expression on his face because she said, "I know it sounds crazy. We thought so too."

Father Cotton sighed as if he had the knowledge of God and too weak a back to support such weight. "It's a madness, I admit, but we all see insanity from afar, but once up close, even the bizarre can seem ordinary."

"I'm beginning to see that," said Patrick. "I need to get back to my boy, Brandon."

Mia, the girl with long brown hair, reacted to that. "Brandon Garter?"

Patrick looked at her. "Yes! You know him?"

"He was in the year above me at school. He was at College for a few months, but left."

Patrick nodded. "Bran joined the family building firm. Were you a...?"

Mia's eyes went wide. "A girlfriend? No way, Brandon was totally weird. Oh, sorry."

"It's all right. Brandon has... issues. That's why I need to get back to him. He's with Tom and Sophie, and a girl named Stacey."

Gwen's eyes went wide. "You saw Stacey?"

He nodded. "Yeah. I pulled the poor mare out of the mud. Why isn't she with you?"

"She was," stated Mia.

"I was unable to save the girl," said Father Cotton regretfully. "When I found Gwen and Mia, they were standing outside the house beneath the bridge, disorientated and panicked. I pulled them beneath the silt and brought them to my sanctuary—as I attempted to do with your friend, Tom, and as I succeeded in doing with you—but Stacey was still inside the house. I cannot enter that foul place."

Patrick stared at the priest, a small man with a slight frame. "Those hands coming out of the ground were you?"

Father Cotton shook his head, eyes glistening. "The damned souls of my parishioners. They aid me when needed. We are not evil. I led the men and women in my congregation astray, and if I could absolve their sins would, but I lost my link to Heaven when I orchestrated the execution of an innocent woman."

"Emily?"

He nodded. "Emily is part of the reason we are here. With her final words she cursed the village of Abbeydale, and inside the web of Martha and Jonathan's darkness, her wishes caught aflame. Her anger and betrayal were so absolute that she was able to cast a dark spell over the village through sheer force of will. Martha and Jonathan had hoped for great rewards from the Great Toad, but instead they found themselves cast down into ruination with the rest of us. If they ever escape this place, their dark bond will renew and their ills upon the world would be felt for the remainder of history. Almost a hundred children died due to their wicked machinations, but their deaths were a mere build up to something greater. Emily's execution was to be their final atrocity before ascendance to immense power—their great offering to Chordaxis. Ironically, it was Emily's dying curse that kept them from their goal."

"Good on the lass," said Patrick. "Tell me how I can get to my boy."

Father Cotton patted Patrick's knee. "I cannot sense your son, which is how I know he is at the house beneath the bridge."

"How do I get there?"

Gwen moaned. "We almost never got out of that place. I wouldn't be in such a rush."

Patrick grunted. He had only one intention, and that was getting to Brandon, so why wouldn't they help him? He sensed Gwen wanted to say more, so he remained quiet and let her.

"We found the house after days of walking," she said. "So, when we saw the little brick house, we made a run for it. We thought we were saved!" She shook her head and blushed. "Stupid! Anyway, inside, we found a fireplace and some chairs. No telephone or anything to help us though. After getting our strength back, we knew we had to keep searching for rescue, and that the house was empty. But Stacey spotted a trapdoor."

"It was creepy," said Mia. "I was too scared to go down."

Gwen nodded. "Me too. Stacey said she'd check out the cellar on her own while we kept watch. I think she was just as scared as us, but didn't want to admit it. Stacey always had to prove how tough she was."

Patrick wondered why she used the past tense. Her friend wasn't dead. "Then what happened?"

"She disappeared. We kept calling out to her, but there was only silence."

"After a while, we both agreed to go down after her," said Mia, "but I wish we hadn't."

Patrick leant forward. "What did you find in the cellar?"

Gwen shook her head. "A nightmare."

☙❧

EVERY TIME TOM WOKE UP RECENTLY, THINGS WERE MORE messed up. Opening his eyes now, the pain in the back of his head and the burning in his right palm told him things were unlikely to improve. Jonathan had stabbed him and pushed him into the cellar.

But why?

And why had Stacey hit Sophie.

Was she a part of this whole thing? Had she lied about being part of the car crash? Was she one of them?

One of whom?

As his mind shifted back and forth, he pictured Sophie falling sideways into the cellar. Was that where they were now? It was dark, and it certainly smelt like a cellar—musky and stale—but he could barely see his hands in front of his face. Probably for the best considering his right hand now had a hole in it.

"Soph? Soph, are you there?"

His question was met with moaning—Sophie's voice. The ground beneath him was cold and unforgiving as he crawled upon it. His skewered right palm throbbed, and his head pulsed with firing cannon blasts. How much more could his body take?

Each time he blinked, the darkness turned a little greyer, and he began to make out shapes. A bulbous object lay right in his path, and when his hands reached out and touched it, he knew exactly what it was. He felt the warmth of a body.

"Hey," Tom whispered, pawing at the body in the dark. "Hey, Soph, is that you?"

The body moaned. It was not Sophie.

"Brandon?"

"Tom?"

"Yeah, it's me. What happened?"

It took a moment for Brandon to reply, like he was coming to. He was still difficult to understand thanks to his ruined tongue, but he spoke slowly and that compensated just enough.

"T-that bitch! I'll slash her fucking throat and fuck her skull."

Tom was taken back by the sudden ferocity, but he supposed the kid had the right. "Tell me what happened, Brandon."

"Stacey smacked me round the head right after she hit you, and Jonathan threw me in the cellar."

So they were in the cellar. What was the deal? Why had Jonathan and Emily been so intent on getting them down here? Was the plan just to keep them prisoner? What would achieve?

Sophie moaned again, bringing Tom back to the situation at hand. "Soph! It's okay, I'm here. Where are you?"

"Tom? Tom... Where are you?"

"Here," he said, pawing around in the darkness. "I'm right here."

"Tom, please? Where are you?"

He could hear her panicking. To keep her calm, he kept talking, using his voice to soothe her. As best he was able, he followed her moans, but it was difficult keeping in a straight line with no light. His hand struck upon something—fleshy and moist. "Soph? Is that you?"

She moaned further away. Whatever Tom had his fingers on was not his wife. He used both hands to pat and prod at the cold, wet obstacle, and tried to build an image in his mind. His hands searched higher, feeling out the shape of a limb—a leg or an arm.

Then he felt bristles. Hardening flesh, less human and more...

Insect?

Too moist.

Tom's heart faltered as a grimness descended upon him. He detected breathing—wet, rapid pants of an animal. Something slithered across the back of his right hand—a hot tongue licking at his stab wound. He clambered to his knees in a panic and strained to see what he was up against, but there was so much darkness.

Nothing but black.

Yellow eyes opened and stared at him.

The animal shrieked, and Tom answered it with his own. It cut short as something struck him hard in the stomach and knocked him down. The back of his head struck the stone floor and more cannon blasts fired in his skull.

"What's going on?" Brandon cried out.

"Tom!" screamed Sophie. "Tom! Where are you?"

He heard the sound of her Zippo lighter flicking open.

Chink!

Click!

A flame appeared and summoned a sphere of light amongst the shadows. Tom saw Sophie cowering in a corner, but before he could get to her, something slithered through the shadows and blocked his way.

"The fuck was that?" Brandon shouted. "The fuck was that?"

Tom didn't know. The thing was pasty and white, its skin glistening briefly in the light of Sophie's lighter. Now it was gone, back in the shadows. Tom scurried towards Sophie, and the two of them embraced. He patted her down, looking for injuries.

"Are you okay?"

"Just my head hurts. Stacey hit me."

"I know. We'll find out why later. First, we have to get out of this fucking cellar."

The creature slithered in the darkness, the slapping sounds it made echoing off the walls. Brandon cried out for help.

"Hold on, Brandon," said Tom. "Just stay right where you are."

"There's something down here with us."

"I know!" He turned to Sophie. "I need the lighter to see with."

She could barely hold it still, so handed it over without argument. Tom moved the flame in front of him, waving it back and forth to try and catch another glimpse of the creature in the dark. No doubt in his mind that it would try to kill them. Perhaps that was why they'd been thrown down here—an offering to whatever foul thing dwelt in the cellar.

They were food.

Bleeding and unarmed.

Prey.

Something brushed past Tom's knee and jolted him into action. He hurried to the side of the room, bashing an elbow against the wall when he reached its end. Exploring with his hand, he felt only cold wet stone. But then, as he followed a line of mortar with his fingers, he felt something less frigid. Some kind of cloth.

The idea of setting a fire came to him disturbingly fast, and before he knew he was doing it, he lifted the lighter and ignited the cloth. It was damp, so the flame started coyly, but once it caught hold it spread vigorously. The darkness retreated as flickering light took over.

The nightmare revealed itself.

The cellar's far corner was piled high with bones—thousands upon thousands of them, and the moisture on the walls was blood, seeping from the stone like sweat. Tom stepped away from the flames and saw a pair of moth-eaten drapes above a stone altar cluttered with strange relics.

Brandon lay in the exact centre of the room, too terrified to even scream as a great beast crouched over him. Tom reacted again, tossing the lighter and grabbing the heaviest thing he could find on the altar, which turned out to be a clay pot. When he lifted it, a knot of toads spilled out, but revulsion was the least of his worries. He launched the pot, and it struck the monster's horned skull and shattered into pieces. Distracted more than hurt, the creature turned on Tom and snarled.

Tom got his first full view of the monstrosity they were trapped with.

Its massive maw lacked teeth, but was wide enough to swallow a human head. Its eyes bulged beneath a pair of stunted horns and its flesh was a mixture of scales and slick skin.

The monster pounced.

Tom ducked, threw himself to the ground.

Massive talons scraped the stone wall deeply enough to leave behind gouges. Tom had rolled to safety with milliseconds to spare. The monster leapt again, never tiring, and each time Tom rolled to safety by the skin of his teeth. All the while, the ancient drapes burned. The cellar grew hotter.

While Tom kept the monster at bay, Brandon dragged himself towards Sophie. She grabbed him beneath his arms and helped him into the corner furthest away from the fire. The only thing keeping Tom alive was that the creature was so gangly. With its long limbs and bulbous body, every attack was preceded by the bending of its legs. He always had just enough time to dodge away.

It was only a matter of time though. Even now, he was growing tired, his dodges getting a little harder to perform each time. He scrambled to the altar, looking for a weapon. The flames made it difficult to keep his eyes open, and some of the items on the altar were already growing hot, but he kept on looking.

The creature shifted in the shadows hesitantly—it did not like the fire either—which meant he had a few seconds while the thing emboldened itself. Items spilled from the altar as he frantically rummaged, and he burned his hands without caring, discarding bones and small clay pots until he found something of use—a torch. It was one of the old-fashioned ones you saw in mediaeval films. The kind people place into holders on the walls of a keep. An odd thing to find, but he didn't question it. He grabbed the torch and held it up to the burning drapes. The flames leapt to it hungrily.

The creature—the giant toad—had gotten over its aversion to fire because it prepared to pounce, but Tom surprised it by leaping first. He thrust the flaming torch into its face, aiming for the pale-yellow eyes. The creature shied away, but couldn't move far. The flames licked at the underside of its maw. A stench of burning flesh filled the cellar.

The creature sprang into the air, screeching and catching Tom in the face with one of its long hind legs, which knocked the burning torch from his hands. He felt his nose break and was suddenly blind as his eyes filled with tears.

"Tom!" Sophie screamed.

He palmed at his eyes, trying to see. His knees threatened to buckle, but he fought to stay standing. The creature rose above him, four feet taller than he. Its maw opened, preparing to swallow its next meal, and Tom was too beaten and disorientated to dodge out of the way this time. He knew enough to not even try.

No point fighting it.

The creature's yellow eyes simmered with hatred. Tom saw his own fear reflected back at him.

The creature pounced.

Brandon appeared, dragging himself along on one elbow and waving the burning torch Tom had dropped on the floor. From on the ground, the kid thrust the torch up underneath the creature's soft underbelly. It let out a screech even louder than before and exploded in a puff of cloying green mist. The mist then turned to a torrent, and toads struck the ground one after another before leaping off in all directions and disappearing between the cracks in the cellar.

Tom stood there amongst the flames and shadows, frozen stiff.

"Did you hear that thing scream?" said Brandon, still on his back. "I really hurt it!"

Sophie rushed over, but didn't seem relieved. "The fire," she said.

Flames were everywhere, creeping along the drapes and licking at the ceiling beams overhead. The trapdoor lay off in the far corner with the ladder leading up to it already reduced to cinders.

"We're trapped down here," said Tom. "We're going to burn."

Sophie searched the room frantically, but the only things were the altar and a huge pile of bones.

"Sophie, get back from the flames. Our only chance is to stay in the centre of the room."

"No!" she shouted back, leaning over the altar. The heat coming off it made the air shimmer. She had to shield her face, but wouldn't come away. Her hair started to smoke, and when she finally backed off, Tom was confused by what she was holding.

"Where the hell did you find that?"

Sophie pulled the pin on the fire extinguisher and let rip. The water came out in a thin, powerful stream, striking the stone walls and turning the fire to steam. The flames flickered anxiously, seeming to know that their mortal enemy had arrived.

"Don't forget the roof beams," Brandon shouted. Lying on his back gave him a good view of the inferno taking hold above.

Sophie swivelled and aimed the extinguisher, killing the roof fire before it had chance to get going. Then she turned back to the drapes.

The room became muggy, hot moisture filling the air, but as the fire retreated the temperature declined back towards tolerable. Now the biggest annoyance was the black ash floating in the already dusty air of the cellar. Tom struggled to breathe through his broken nose, so he knelt on the floor and exhaled into his cupped hands. Brandon dragged himself up beside him.

"What was that thing?"

"I have no idea, but it looked like some kind of toad, except... worse."

"We're proper fucked, ain't we?"

Tom nodded. "We were fucked the moment we drove across that bridge. We just didn't know it."

"It was my fault."

Tom frowned. "What do you mean?"

"The crash was my fault. I didn't tie down the shovels in the back of our truck. When my dad stood on the brake, they launched across the bridge and hit your car."

Tom replayed the memory—the image of Soph with her neck sliced open by a shovel. It had smashed through their windshield and caused everything. "We're all fucking doomed because of you? You little shit!"

Brandon was helpless. His right leg was a limp hunk of meat and pain had left him exhausted, but that didn't stop Tom from leaping on the kid and pummelling him with lefts and rights. Brandon cried out and put his hands over his face to protect himself, so when Tom's blows stopped getting through he swivelled and punched the kid's broken shin instead. That got Brandon wailing a pleasing tune.

"You piece of shit!" he screamed in the kid's face. "You fucked us all."

Sophie dragged Tom off. "What the hell are you doing!"

"He caused the crash, Soph. He fucking admitted it." Breaking free of her grasp, he booted Brandon in his broken leg, drawing more screams. Sophie dragged Tom away again, this time locking her wrists around his waist.

"Calm down, Tom!"

"He did this to us, Soph! He's the one who kill-"

"I don't care who caused the crash, Tom! What does it matter? None of us is to blame for being stuck here. How could Brandon have known we'd end up in this place?"

"I'm sorry," Brandon sobbed, clutching his leg. "I wanted to tell you at the beginning."

Tom tried so hard to unclench his fists, but just couldn't. Only he had the image of Sophie nearly decapitated by one of Brandon's shovels. Only he had felt her death as if it were real. Rationally, however, he knew she was right. The crash had been an unfortunate accident happening at the worst place—a cursed place.

He managed to unclench his fists and placed out his palms to show peace. "Okay," he said. "All right."

Sophie released her grip on him and let out a sigh of relief when he remained in place.

"I'm sorry," Brandon.

Brandon blinked tears from his eyes and stared at the ceiling. "Me too."

"But if we don't find a way out of here, I'll kill you."

Sophie went to grab him again. "Tom!"

"No, Soph, I mean it. Keep him away from me."

"How? He can't walk."

Tom wasn't interested in Brandon's problems, at least for the moment. What he wanted to focus on was getting out of this cellar. The trapdoor was unreachable with the ladder reduced to kindling, so the only way out was through the minute cracks the toads had slithered between. They needed something to help them. Like when they'd had to put out the fire.

He turned to Sophie. "How did you find an extinguisher? I searched that altar and there was nothing there but bones and pots."

Sophie frowned. "It was right there, plain as day. How did you not see it?"

"It's weird," said Brandon, eyeing Tom warily to see if he would let him speak. "Everything in this house—this cellar—is old. Even Jonathan was all old-timey. It's like we slipped into the past."

Tom nodded. "I agree. This house—whatever this place is—is from Jonathan's time, not ours. That fire extinguisher has no place here."

"Then how did I get it?" Sophie asked in an irritated tone. She always got annoyed when the sums didn't tally. She did not enjoy being confused.

"The altar," said Tom. "I think we were meant as an offering to that monster—the god of toads, or whatever it was. Maybe the altar grants wishes."

Sophie sniffed. "It didn't look like a genie to me."

"No," said Brandon, "not to me either, but Jonathan kept going on about how the cellar provides whatever a person needs, didn't he? Tom needed a way to fight off the... toad king, so it gave him a way to use fire against it. Sophie, you needed a way to put the fire out before we burned alive. The altar gave you an extinguisher."

"Great," said Sophie, giving a lopsided grin. "Then I'll ask for a teleporter to get us out of here." She marched up to the altar and put both hands on it. "Hello? Toad monster, are you there? Give me a phone with an internet connection and a frappuccino."

Tom frowned. She was making fun, but he thought Brandon was on to something. The altar had given them what they had needed at each time. "You've already had your turn," he said, working things through in his head.

Sophie turned from the altar with her arms folded. "What?"

"You and I already got what we needed. I don't think it gives a second go, at least not without more sacrifices. Maybe Jonathan intended to take from the altar after offering us to the monster, but we used it instead. If there's one wish for each of us, then Brandon still has a turn."

"I want a way out of here," said Brandon, propped up on his elbow. "Carry me over and I'll fix this."

Tom stepped towards Brandon and the kid flinched, so he held his palms out. "Truce, okay? I'm just going to help you up."

Brandon nodded and allowed Tom to pull him up onto his one good leg. The smell of stale blood and sweat wafted from the kid and made Tom queasy. Sophie helped, and between them they got the kid to the altar.

"Do I close my eyes?" he asked.

"I didn't," said Tom. "I just searched for what I needed."

Sophie nudged him. "Tom, look!" She was motioning to one side of the altar, and when Tom saw what was there, he groaned.

Brandon saw the items too and huffed. "Guess they're for me."

"Well, you can't say it hasn't given him what he needs," said Sophie, sounding amused if nothing else.

"Yes," said Tom, "but nothing that will help the rest of us. We're still screwed."

Brandon reached out and took his gifts. "Less screwed than we were though, admit it."

CHAPTER 11

Brandon had spent the last thirty minutes screwing around on the aluminium crutches in the light of Tom's torch. He took a while to get the rhythm right, but was now zipping about like a bug. *Click clack click clack.*

Sophie thought it was a sick trick, like the movie she had watched about a cursed monkey paw during one of her many evenings alone while Tom worked. In that movie, the monkey's paw had granted people's wishes, but always in some twisted misinterpretation that did nothing but increase the wisher's misery. The altar had helped Brandon, but only by giving him crutches. True, it was what the kid needed, but seriously...

Where was her goddamn teleporter?

Tom sat against the wall beneath the unreachable trapdoor. She had watched the hope leak out of him in the last half-hour. Since they'd woken up on the riverbed—what seemed like an eternity ago now—he had been forced to act strong, to fight, and to think of solutions. Now, he had nothing to do but ruminate. His busy mind had fallen idle, and the only thing to fill it was despair. Tom had always been prone to depression. Ever since first failing to get his wife pregnant.

God, she hated him so much.

And yet she loved him.

Hated how self-involved he could be. Loved how hard he tried.

Hated how blind he could be. Loved how he knew her better than she knew herself.

Hated that she loved him so much. Loved that she loved him so much.

She had to get out of this place. This couldn't be the end of her life. Not this. Not halfway between her old life and her new. As much as the thought of leaving Tom hurt her, it also filled her with excitement. Her life was no longer set in stone. There were new surprises in her future.

But not if this nightmare didn't end.

"Okay, Tom," she said. "We have to figure something out. You're sat here doing nothing, and that's not you."

He looked up at her through bleary eyes, nose swollen making him resemble a cat. She couldn't even bear looking at his ruined right hand. "I've been wracking my brain, Soph. I have nothing left."

She folded her arms. "What do we do when the figures don't add up, when we've been over them a million times, and they just won't behave?"

He frowned at her. "We... go back to the client and ask questions."

"Yes! We go back to the source."

"What are you saying?"

"I'm saying that Jonathan threw us down here, and he can get us out."

Tom tutted. "Why would he help us?"

"He wanted our help to kill the blind monk, and before he betrayed us, he acted like he was a good guy, a hero. But his sums didn't add up, and you questioned him. Let's question him some more. The only way we're getting out of here is if somebody upstairs helps us. It's the best shot we have. It's the only shot we have."

"What do you propose?"

Sophie looked up at the trapdoor. Then she screamed. "JONATHAN! JONATHAN, WE NEED YOUR HELP. HELP US!"

Brandon flinched and wobbled on his crutches. "Jeez!"

Sophie realised Tom was watching her in awe. It was unlike her to take charge, but it was something she had been doing more and more lately as she faced her impending independence. She didn't need Tom to take care of her anymore. She would bloody well help herself.

"JONATHAN! WE HAVE SOMETHING YOU NEED. HELP US, AND WE WILL HELP YOU!"

To her surprise the trapdoor opened. She'd envisioned the plan working, but only after several hours of screaming. This seemed too easy.

Jonathan peered down at her, the shock obvious on his face. "You live?"

"We took care of your God," she shouted.

Jonathan gawped in silence. Then, "Why are you shouting?"

"I want to make a deal."

"Ha! Chordaxis shall return soon and devour you. Then I shall pray at the altar and receive my rewards."

"What rewards? You're stuck here like the rest of us."

He smiled at this, like he knew something she did not. He probably knew lots she didn't, but he was still just a man, and men could be tempted. Sophie chided herself for being judgemental and reminded herself that women could be tempted too. But not today. Today she would not be the fairer sex.

"We've already had the altar's rewards, sorry. I've got something that can help you."

A flash of emotion gave Jonathan away, but he fought to remain stone-faced. "What could you possibly have received to help me?"

Sophie laughed like he was an idiot. She hoped he was. "A way out." Even at a distance, she saw his jaw tighten. "Get us out of this cellar, and the item is yours."

"And why would I not kill you immediately after receiving it?"

"Because we'll take care of the blind monk for you. He'll try to stop you leaving, right? So why risk having him around during your one chance of escape?"

Again, Jonathan tightened his jaw before answering. "Why the change of mind?"

Sophie lost her composure. "Because I want out of this fucking hellhole. You said if we kill the monk, we can leave. Is that true, or were you fudging the figures?"

"I don't know what that means, but yes, the monk is part of the spell placed upon Abbeydale by the righteous, self-serving monks at the abbey. To kill the blind monk would be to break the tether keeping this place in existence. You could escape that way, yes, but why bother if you say you have another way out?"

Sophie had to think fast. She thought about Brandon's crutches and the way the altar liked to give a person just enough to help them. "It isn't our way out, it's your way out. I need to get out of this cellar, and the altar gave me what I needed—a way to bargain with you and get us out of here."

Jonathan stared at her, and she stared right back. The first to look away would weaken their position.

It won't be me, matey. I'm pushing this transaction through whether you like it or not. I will not blink.

Jonathan looked away. He sat at the edge of the trapdoor for many minutes, and Sophie remained quiet the whole time. The fact he was even thinking about it meant they would make a deal—it was just a question of who got the better end of it.

Jonathan grunted. "You really have something I can use to leave this place? Show it to me."

"No! You let us out this hole and it's yours, but no way am I taking it out my pocket until then."

"You're lying!"

"No, I'm not."

"Then why won't you simply show it to me?"

Sophie laughed. "Because I don't trust this place, and I don't trust you. For all I know, you'll magic it right out of my hand. I'll feel safer keeping it out of sight until we're back up top. You wouldn't understand what it does, anyway. It's from my time, not yours."

Jonathan pulled a face, but then he huffed. The man could not fight his curiosity. "Fine. Wait there."

"Where else am I going to go?"

A minute passed. Jonathan returned with a bundle of rope and threw one end down the hole. "What are we supposed to do with that?" Sophie asked.

"It is all I have. Use it or do not."

Brandon shook his head. "I can't climb that."

"You don't have to," she told him. "I'll tie a harness around you and Jonathan will lift you from above."

"I shall try," Jonathan corrected. "I am but one man."

Sophie sneered. "Why don't you get Stacey to help you?"

"She serves another," was his reply. "Shall we make progress?"

Sophie got to work, tying the generous length of rope around Brandon's crotch and waist, holding him in place with a makeshift rope basket. He threw his new crutches across his lap and nodded to communicate that he was ready.

She gave the rope a tug and felt it was taut. "Okay, send him up."

Jonathan disappeared, but the sound of him straining stayed behind. Brandon cried out as the rope dragged him forward a step on his splinted leg, but then he was rising upwards, leaving the flickering light and entering the canopy of shadows. Progress was slow. It was a good thing Stacey wasn't there to help because Sophie was more than a little pissed with her.

Tom stood nearby and whispered. "What are you going to do when he asks for the item you promised?"

"Give him something else," she said, shrugging.

Glad of the darkness, she went over to the corner where the mountain of bones stood—the toad king's leftovers. Once her foot struck against the pile's bottom, she reached down into the shadows and grasped about. She wanted a bone that was small and sharp and selected a shard not unlike a tiny dagger—easy to conceal in the pocket where she'd pretended to keep the fictitious item promised to Jonathan. It was the best plan she could put together, and better than being stuck in this cellar.

It took several minutes, but Brandon eventually clawed his way through the hatch. Sophie called up to him to check he was okay.

"Yeah," he replied, although the discomfort was obvious in his voice. "It's all clear up here."

"Okay," said Sophie. "Drop the rope back down."

The rope came back, and she nodded to Tom. Tom shook his head. "I'm not leaving you down here."

"I'll be fine, now go." She leant forward to whisper the next part. "Once he knows I have nothing, you won't be able to climb up, so I have to go last."

He looked like he would argue, but gave in and took the rope with a simple grunt. She helped him up by shoving him under the butt—the most intimate they'd been in a year.

"Promise you'll buy me dinner later," he said, but his delivery was ruined by exertion. Sophie watched him ascend towards the hatch, leaving her alone in the dank cellar. The torch still burned on the ground, giving her light to see by, but beyond its fiery glow was unrelenting darkness.

She almost didn't see it when the shadows moved.

The lonely toad hopped towards her and put dread in her bones. When she saw several more emerge, she knew the monster that lived there was returning.

And this time she was alone.

She grabbed the flaming torch and used it to part the shadows. The light revealed hundreds of leaping toads all moving towards her. She looked up at the hatch and cried out. "Tom? Would you mind getting a move on?"

"I'm... going as... fast—"

"Well go faster," she hollered. A toad brushed her foot, making her stamp around in a panic, and she almost slipped when her foot came down on the slimy back of a fat little critter. She rescued her balance and crushed as many as she could, but even with the risk of obliteration they kept on coming.

Surrounding her.

Another toad brushed her foot. She looked down and saw a fat, bulldog-like thing not much smaller than a bowling ball. She went to kick it, but it jerked and bit down on her ankle. The pain was immense, like being pierced by a dozen tiny needles.

Tom made it through the trapdoor above and threw the rope back down. "Your turn, Soph."

She had tried to keep herself from screaming, but now asked herself why. Realising there was no reason to be quiet, she took the rope between her legs and bellowed. She tried to dislodge the monstrous toad biting her ankle, but it wouldn't let go. More and more of the slimy critters broke from the shadows and there was no way to defend herself as she invested herself fully in climbing.

The toads hit her body all over with thunderous jabs, but only the bulldog toad bit her. It still clung to her ankle defiantly, but

Sophie kept her focus on the square of light above her and worked as fast as she could to get there. She chanced a single glance below and saw the toads piling up beneath her, higher and higher—becoming something else.

The toad king was reforming. And it was angry.

Tom realised something was wrong. "Soph, what is it?"

"Pull faster," she shouted hysterically. "Must pull faster."

"Okay, okay."

Sophie's ascent increased speed, and the massive toad on her ankle finally fell away. She climbed as fast as she was able, but Tom did most of the work now that he knew she was in danger. Beneath her, the angry abomination hissed. She couldn't help but glance down again, immediately wishing she hadn't.

The toad king was back, and its massive hind legs were folded up ready to spring. It would drag her right back down into the darkness.

"Get me up, Tom! Get me up! Get me up!"

Tom pulled faster, crying out with exertion. She stopped climbing, frozen stiff by fear—from the anticipation of being snatched back into darkness. Away from safety.

Away from her husband.

"Tom!"

Sophie closed her eyes and thought of the day she had married Tom—a happy day. A day when her entire life had promised to be joyful. She'd loved him so much back then, read vows of her own making, and now, as she awaited death, she considered how much she still loved him. That she would never get to hold him again made her heart ache.

She felt the air move beneath her, something rising. A beast coming to claim her.

"I'm sorry, Tom."

She felt the air move as the monster leapt from its pit and rose up to devour her.

"Don't be sorry," said Tom, yanking her up out of the hatch and into his sweaty arms. "But you can be grateful. I'm about to pass out. Jesus!"

Sophie looked back at the hatch and saw something slice through the shadows beneath. Jonathan kicked the trapdoor closed, and the nightmare ended. She was safe. Without thinking, she kissed Tom on the mouth, more passionately than she ever thought she would. Once the kiss was over, she threw her arms around him and wept. She was tired of being strong. Let him take over again for a while.

"I am grateful," she sobbed. "I'm grateful."

"Where is the item the altar gave to you?" Jonathan demanded. He had his sword unsheathed and pointed it at them. "Hand it over now, or I'll throw you all right back down there."

Tom and Sophie shared a glance. They still had their promise to kill the monk to trade on, but this could get ugly.

"Oh, yeah," said Sophie. "About that..."

Jonathan's face turned crimson, like blood would seep from his eyes any moment. He pointed his sword at Sophie's left eye, making her blink nervously. "Then you die. The other two can trade for their lives, but I don't need the three of you. I never really expected the truth, but I thought it might be fun to see what you would try."

"We deserve points for effort," said Brandon, sitting on a chair nearby with his crutches. His splints were cracked and his leg awash with blood.

"I'm bored with you now." Jonathan raised his sword, a snarl contorting his face as whatever mask of humanity he possessed slipped away to reveal a monster as merciless as the one in the cellar.

Then his head whipped sideways as Brandon hopped from his chair and walloped him with one of his aluminium crutches hard enough to hit a six. Jonathan's eyes rolled back in his head and he collapsed in a heap.

"People really need to start paying more attention to the cripple," said Brandon, hopping on one leg and readjusting his crutches. "Kicking ass gives me a warm glow."

Sophie prodded Tom with her toe. "Let's throw him down the hole," she snarled. "See how he fucking likes it."

"We can't," said Brandon, still hopping on one foot. "He's passed out on top of the hatch, and I don't feel like hanging around to move him."

"Me either," said Tom. "Let's just get out of here."

Sophie shook her head. "No way, we're not leaving. Pick up that rope and tie him up. I am one pissed off accountant, and I want answers."

۞

FATHER COTTON DISAPPEARED INTO THE BACK OF THE CHURCH and returned a few minutes later with piping hot tea. Gwen and Mia seemed unimpressed by the hot drink, but Patrick thought it was the best thing he'd ever tasted.

"You've really been down here for days?" he asked the girls.

Mia nodded. "My mum will go mad."

"Let's not worry about your mum, Mia," said Gwen. "And I don't think we've been down here for days in the real sense. Maybe we're still trapped in the split-second we crashed."

"I don't know the truth of it," Father Cotton interjected. "I have been here so long I barely remember the other place."

Patrick glanced around the homely church, but channelled his vision on the thick wooden doors that opened onto that wretched place that made no sense. "The world has got its problems, Father, but I would quite like to get back there. My old lady will have put the supper on."

"And I would see it so."

"So, what do I need to do?"

"What do we need to do," corrected Gwen. "We've been going over it with Father Cotton since we got here. We need to go back to the house."

Patrick nodded. "The house where your friend Stacey was attacked by some kind of frog thing?"

"A toad," Father Cotton corrected. "Chordaxis."

"Yeah, that sod. What is he doing in a cellar?"

Father Cotton waved an arm, indicating the interior of his church. "As God provided a sanctuary for his followers, so did Chordaxis provide a sanctuary for his. The house is a den of evil, and the home of the toad."

"So, it's a haunted house with a monster in the basement. Splendid."

Father Cotton chided him with a look. "Not a monster, a

demon. A creature of immense evil, responsible for many of the world's ills during my time. His influence causes greed, and his followers yearn for wealth and power at any cost."

"Don't need a demon to cause that," said Patrick. "It's human nature."

"Perhaps," Father Cotton admitted. "All the same, Chordaxis is a foe of all who walk in the light. He is weak now, having not fed on enough souls to sustain him, but at his mightiest he can bend the strongest minds to his will—make powerful men lust after more than they should. Leaders and monarchs will fall to ruin and take their people with them."

"Not many monarchs left," said Patrick, "but so-called leaders we have in spades. You don't want this thing let out of its cellar, huh? So how do we escape without having it follow us?"

"Emily's curse keeps the wicked contained here, a punishment for me and the others who wronged her, but it is Chordaxis and his minions, Martha and Jonathan, who trap the innocent here. Their snare drags souls like yours here so that the toad may feed and grow strong. Strong enough to dispel Emily's curse and leave here. It is their way out, and if allowed to happen, the beast will resume its corruption of mankind. Martha and Jonathan will serve as fervent acolytes." He stopped for a moment to chuckle. "The day we burned Emily alive we did the world a great service, because in her fury, she plunged that wicked trio into the abyss right alongside the villagers who betrayed her."

"So, if Chordaxis eats enough souls, the whole world is screwed?" Patrick was smiling, but he didn't find it funny.

Father Cotton nodded. "He has eaten many over the years, but never so many as what he could do so now with all of you arriving here at once. Your companions—"

"My son!"

"It may already be too late for him, but the riverbed is still barren, and therefore, I do not think the toad has eaten all what it must. Emily's spell is still intact."

Patrick clutched at hope. "Or my son and the others are still alive, and your toad demon hasn't eaten at all yet. Maybe they're okay."

Father Cotton sighed and relented. "Perhaps, but that was not true for Stacey. When she eventually left the house beneath the bridge, she was without a soul. Martha had stitched her mouth closed with a toad inside, a way of keeping her husk under control, but all that she was had been consumed by Chordaxis. I buried the girl in the mud, hoping to contain her there while I saw to Gwen and Mia, but it seems she escaped."

"With my help," Patrick groaned. "She seemed like a frightened young girl to me."

"Martha's influence. Stacey is nothing but a puppet now, an echo of a previous life. Her soul has been consumed, and she suffers with the villagers of Abbeydale. Their screams are the fuel that empowers him. If he is able to consume more..."

"Yeah, I got you, Father. Stop banging on about it. I am ready to go find my boy. Getting him to safety is in line with what you want, so you have no reason not to help me."

"It isn't that easy," said Mia. "We need to kill Chordaxis if we have any chance of getting out of here."

"So, I'll kill the bugger. Wouldn't be the pest I've stepped on."

"He is a demon, not vermin," said Father Cotton. "And you would do well not to take him lightly. If you confront the beast, you must do so wisely, and as a unified force."

"We're coming with you," said Gwen. Mia nodded beside her.

"And what about you?" Patrick asked the priest.

Father Cotton looked down at his hands clasped in his lap. "You forget what I become when I step outside the light. While I have modest control over my actions, my monstrous nature makes me too dangerous to be around. It would not be long before I tried to kill you. Also, I told you Emily's spell is focused on me. If I am to die in battle, Chordaxis would find an alternative route to the world. If I die, so does Emily's curse. You see, Chordaxis has two ways of succeeding, while we barely have one. The demon cannot be killed."

Patrick threw his arms up hopelessly. "Then what are we even talking about?"

"We are talking about killing the toad king's acolytes. Kill them and the toad loses its ability to feed. He cannot move within the sphere of Emily's curse, only inside his dungeon. Without his acolytes to bring him souls, he will starve and go into hibernation.

There is a reason no villagers remain here, Patrick. Over time, Martha and Jonathan have taken them all and fed their souls to the toad. This church used to have a congregation. My, it was wonderful."

"Then why hasn't Chordaxis become powerful enough to leave?"

"Because the people of Abbeydale were damned, and damned souls can only sustain the beast, not empower it. Chordaxis needs innocent blood like yours to grow strong."

Patrick huffed. "I'm not innocent."

"Have you ever killed anybody? Raped anybody? Stolen from someone more needy than you?"

"No, of course not! But... I have done things."

"So have all men, Patrick, and God forgives all but the worst. The souls of Abbeydale were beyond redemption and provided mere morsels for the beast to feed upon. It is you and your companions the toad needs to escape this place."

"Wonderful," said Patrick. "So, what do the three of us need to do? I don't have the body to be a hero."

Father Cotton got up from the pews. "The first thing you need to do is listen carefully, but first I shall fetch us more tea."

"Make mine a strong one," said Patrick.

"I'm afraid I only have decaf."

"Jesus Christ," said Patrick. "This really is Hell."

CHAPTER 12

T om thought he would die in that cellar. Now he was up top he felt little better. Once again, the house had changed, and it now resembled a narrow, stone cottage. No fireplace this time, but a stove-pipe furnace stood on three legs in the corner. As before, enough chairs existed for each person and no more.

Sophie already sat, and she glared at Jonathan who was beginning to stir. Tom put his hand on her shoulder and asked what she planned to do. She'd calmed in the last few minutes, but he could see she was a bag of nerves.

"Thought I'd try my hand at torture," she said. "I suppose the professionals call it 'interrogation'."

"Usually I'd argue against such nefarious means, but in this case..." He sneered at Jonathan, the man who had attempted to feed them to a monster, and said, "I say he has it coming."

"I can do the torture part if you'd like," said Brandon, leaning up against the wall on his crutches. The kid's eager tone was unsettling, and the act of tying Jonathan up had seemed to revitalise him. He noticed the disturbed looks they gave him and shrugged. "I mean, if you don't have the stomach for it."

"And you do?" Tom asked.

Brandon looked at Jonathan hungrily and nodded. The kid really wanted his revenge. Who could blame him?

"It's okay, Brandon," said Tom. "We're all in this together, so let's just see what happens."

Jonathan muttered something and lifted his head.

"He's about to wake up," said Sophie. She reached out and took Tom's hand. "Are you with me?"

He put his head against hers. "Of course. We're not divorced yet."

"Maybe never," she said.

"Don't say things you don't mean."

"But I—"

"No! We're both scared out of our minds and in a lot of trouble. It's only natural we've buried the hatchet for now, but I know if we get out of this alive, you'll still leave me, Soph."

She looked hurt. "We both made the decision."

Tom took a step back. For a second, he wanted to slap her, to show her how angry and upset she'd made him over the last few months, but he would never do that—could never hurt her in that way. That didn't mean he wasn't pissed off though.

"It was a decision led by you, Soph, and ratified by me as a formality. What was I supposed to say when you announced you wanted a divorce? There was no way I could convince you to stay with me once you'd reached that point. What I blame you for most is not telling me how unhappy you were a year ago—or two."

"I tried!"

"But I'm not a mind reader, Soph. Subtle hints don't cut the mustard for this. I needed the facts, and you kept them to yourself."

They were waltzing into a shouting match, he could see the footwork lining up, but instead of trying to take the lead, Sophie retreated. "You're right," she said. "I never gave you enough of a chance to change. In my mind, it is painful enough you've changed from the man I married. If I have to tell you to act differently, then it doesn't count, it's not good enough. I want you to cherish me without having to tell you."

"I do cherish you, Soph. How can you not see that?"

"Because I'm not a mind reader."

End of argument. As much as he blamed her for not telling him she was unhappy, how guilty was he for not telling her how he felt about her? How often had he showed her how much she still meant to him? Hell, when was the last time he had even bought her flowers? He had taken her love for granted—like it was an asset he owned—but it hadn't been an asset, it had been an investment. One he'd let sink.

Jonathan cackled. He lifted his head to study them, and his opaque dead eyes took them all by surprise.

"Wow!" said Brandon, rattling on his crutches. "What's with his eyes? Looks like they came out of a corpse."

Tom felt the milky white orbs drilling into his soul. Fish hooks tugged at his guts. "What are you, Jonathan?"

Jonathan stopped laughing and stared at Tom like a malicious child examining an ant before he stepped on it. "I am the end of all things. The enslaver of mankind. The right hand of the Great Darkness that beats in mankind's bosom."

"That toad thingy?" mocked Brandon.

"Chordaxis!" Jonathan spat furiously. "The devourer of worlds. But yes... the toad thingy."

Tom frowned. "That monster couldn't even devour me! Let alone the world."

"There is no failure for that which is eternal. My master is weakened, yes, but growing stronger all the time. Now that you are all here..." he looked around the room and cackled again. "Soon you shall be nothing more than shattered fragments of that which you were. You shall be a fine feast for my master."

"Nice," said Sophie. "Or maybe I'll step on the slimy bugger. I never was one much for wildlife."

Jonathan glared at her. "I shall enjoy draining you of blood. The taste shall be divine."

Sophie kept her stare on Jonathan as she spoke. "Brandon?"

"Yeah?"

"Fetch me Jonathan's sword."

Brandon brought it to her, moving on his crutches like he'd been born with them. Once he handed Sophie the weapon, she looked dangerous, but when Tom studied Jonathan, the man seemed unafraid.

"Why are we here?" She thrust the sword at Jonathan's left eye.

"Because you are damned, wench."

"We are not. We should not be in this place."

"And yet you are, wench."

Tom watched Sophie growing angrier. He wondered if she would actually stab Jonathan.

"How do we leave?" she was demanding now.

Jonathan kept a smirk on his face the entire time. "You do not."

And that was how the conversation continued for several minutes until Sophie finally snapped. She trembled with frustration by the time she leapt up from her chair. Tom took her away and told her to leave the sword with Brandon. Last thing he needed was to end up on the receiving end if he said the wrong thing. Brandon was happy to oblige, and twirled the weapon appreciatively in his hands as they walked away.

Beside the popping furnace, Tom and Sophie conferred. "He isn't afraid of me," she said.

Tom nodded. "I'm not sure he has any reason to be. I'm not even sure he's human. At least not completely."

"His eyes..." Sophie said. "They look dead."

"Maybe he *is* dead. Maybe he feels no pain."

Sophie disagreed. "Brandon knocked him out with his crutch. Jonathan can be hurt, I'm sure of it."

Despite not enjoying the malicious glint in her eyes while she said it, it was a good point and Tom nodded. "You're right. I suppose it's time to put our money where our mouth is."

"I can't," said Sophie, the maliciousness fading away. "I thought I would be able to, but no matter how hard I tried I couldn't use the sword on him. At one point I wanted to put out his goddamn eye, but my hand wouldn't budge an inch."

Tom sighed. Part of him was glad his wife of many years was incapable of blinding someone with a sword, but it didn't help their cause. "I'm not sure I can do it either, but I'll try. We need to get answers. I still don't understand what this place is. If we're in Hell, I would rather know it."

"Me too. If we really are damned, then at least we can settle in and make ourselves at home."

Tom tittered. If they could keep their sense of humour, perhaps things wouldn't be so bad.

There was a scream from the centre of the room. Sophie and

Tom spun around. Brandon had the sword and was pushing it into Jonathan's shoulder.

"What are you!?" he screamed into the man's face, drool hanging from his snarling lower lip. "Tell me!"

"I am a servant of darkness," Jonathan yelled. "And I shall end you."

Brandon pushed the sword in further. "How do we get out of here? Tell me or I'll carve your heart out and eat it in front of you!"

Jonathan wailed in agony as the sword wiggled inside him. "You... you must climb the banks."

"We tried that, asshole. Tell the truth."

"It is... it is the truth. You must climb the banks, but first you must weaken the spell. Kill the monk. Kill the monk and the spell shall be broken. It's like... like I've been telling you all along. Kill the monk. Break the spell."

"If you're lying..." Brandon yanked out the bloody sword and held it against Jonathan's milky left eye.

"I am not lying! Kill the monk and you may leave. I swear it."

Tom pulled Brandon away who stuck the sword in Jonathan and left it there. "All right, kid. Take it down a notch."

Jonathan's neck bulged with pain. "Thought I was supposed to be the evil one."

"I'm getting answers!" Brandon was panting, and Tom detected a hint of arousal in the kid's dreamy expression. What was his deal?

"He did a good job," said Sophie, nodding at Brandon.

"No sweat." Still panting, he stared lustfully at Sophie.

Tom moved in front of his wife. "Yeah, okay, good job, Brandon. I believe what Jonathan said about the monk. The riverbed moved when we tried to climb out. The monk tried to stop us leaving. With him gone, I reckon we can get out."

"So, all we have to do," said Sophie, "is kill a monster."

Tom grunted. "No problem. Jonathan will tell us everything we need to know."

They turned around to verify, but Jonathan was gone.

Tom stomped towards the chair. "Damn it!"

"Where the fuck is he?" Brandon demanded, that look of arousal turning to rage.

Jonathan flew at them from the corner of the room like a

sweeping bat and smashed into Sophie. She collided with Tom and they hit the ground together in a tangle. Jonathan remained airborne, arms stretched out on either side of him. His elbows and wrists started cracking. His fingers lengthened to wicked claws. His face wrenched and distorted as human flesh became glistening scale.

Brandon hopped on one leg and raised both fists. "Come on then!"

Tom tried to grab the kid before he got himself killed. "Brandon, get back."

But it was too late.

Jonathan swept Brandon up like a toddler and lifted him into the air. The timber roof opened into a ragged mouth, revealing a swirling portal of black and red. All air in the cabin vanished.

Sophie screamed. "Brandon!"

Jonathan glared at them from above, a twisted smirk upon his monstrous face. Brandon cried out for help and Jonathan cackled. Then the two of them spiralled upwards and disappeared into the portal.

The roof snapped shut.

Sophie slumped against Tom and released a stream of obscenities. Once she'd finished, she said, "I really hate this place."

"We'll make sure to leave a review after we leave."

Sophie put herself in his arms. She was dirty and bloody, yet somehow calm. "You think we can?"

"What? Leave a review?"

"No, get out of here?"

The truth was Tom didn't know any way out of this, and a good accountant did not guess. The only thing he could do was look on the bright side. He put an arm around Sophie and told her not what he thought, but what he hoped. "If there's a way out of this place, Soph, you and I will find it."

She rose up to face him. "I don't know what is going to happen, Tom, not even in the next few minutes, but this nightmare has made me realise that, no matter what, I don't regret our lives together. I don't regret loving you. And I will never stop loving you." She kissed him on the mouth. "Also, for the time being, we're still husband and wife, so let's show this place that you don't mess with the Sumners."

Tom smiled, and they kissed again.

👁️

THE PLAN WAS AGREED UPON—PATRICK WOULD TRY TO SAVE THE world. He was only playing along at this point because the church was the only place he felt safe since waking up. Father Cotton and the two girls appeared genuine at least, so until otherwise convinced, Patrick would trust them. He couldn't deny things were beyond his own understanding, anyway. The church was likely older and more ancient than anything he could imagine—a living ruin— and Father Cotton was a ghost.

I really need a pint.

Patrick had spent the last thirty minutes sitting alone in the pews, ever since Father Cotton had led Gwen and Mia into a small room off the side of the church. During his solitude, he thought only of Brandon. He did not know if his son was alive or dead, or eternally damned.

When they returned, Gwen and Mia had serene expressions on their faces. Both smiled at Patrick before taking a pew several rows down. Father Cotton continued until he was standing beside Patrick.

"Everything okay, Father?"

"As well as things ever are in this place. It is almost time."

Patrick sighed. "Uh huh."

"If you have anything burdening you, my child, now would be the time to share it."

"Thought you'd forgotten religion, Father?"

The priest gave a slight smile. "I retained my compassion, even if I do not hold the answers to the universe. My days as a practising priest are a memory, but I still recall the strength a man gains when unburdening himself. Step into my vestry, and you may speak your troubles in confidence, Patrick. I will not judge—I shall only listen."

"I have no secrets, Father."

"You do, Patrick. All men do. Share them with me and see

yourself unencumbered. You may not get another chance, and if there is yet another place beyond this one, wouldn't you prefer to leave your worries behind?"

Patrick gripped the pew with both hands and studied the priest. One word kept beating through his skull. 'Brandon, Brandon, Brandon.' He stood up before he even realised he was doing it. "Fine, Father. How do we do this thing?"

"The vestry is at the back of the church."

The two of them walked the aisle, past Gwen and Mia who were holding each other and whispering. Patrick wondered what sins they had freed themselves of to be so peaceful. Were they even old enough to have accrued anything to atone for?

As Father Cotton had said, a small room lay off the side of the church behind the altar. It was barred by a poorly hung wooden door. The priest pushed the door open and revealed a windowless chamber. "Please, take a seat."

Patrick located a pair of stools—essentially a pair of thick tree stumps—and sat down. Father Cotton took the remaining one and patted Patrick's knee. "Now, my child, tell me your biggest worry or your smallest. We shall start at one end and work inward."

"Okay dokay. My biggest problem is that I'm stuck in a hell dimension and still have to go to church. My smallest problem is the boil on my arse cheek."

"This is serious, Patrick."

"You're telling me, I can barely sit down. Would you like a look?"

"No, Patrick, I mean this is serious. I do not wish to see you leave here with unanswered crimes on your conscious. There is enough strife ahead of you, I promise, so please tell me what is on your mind."

"Nothing."

"You are worried about your son?"

"Of course I bloody well am. He's trapped in this place somewhere. Dead or alive."

"Which frightens you most?"

Patrick tutted. "A stupid question."

"Yet, one you didn't answer."

"I want him to be alive. He's my boy. I've been looking out for him his whole life."

"Can the boy not fend for himself?"

"No," grunted Patrick. "He can't."

Father Cotton put his hand back on Patrick's knee and squeezed it. "Why not, my child?"

"Because he belongs in the bleedin' loony bin."

Father Cotton allowed Patrick's statement to hang in the air for a moment, lowering his head as if in prayer. Once the moment had passed, he looked up solemnly and said, "I do not understand what those words mean exactly, so please would you educate me?"

Patrick couldn't believe he'd finally said it. For so long he'd been carrying the secret in his head, convincing himself it wasn't real, and that Brandon was just a normal lad. It was just a phase his boy was going through. He told himself that again and again. But it hadn't been a phase, had it? Normal teenagers did not enjoy the things Brandon did.

"He's not right in the head, Father. A fruitcake. Does that make sense to you?"

"Enough sense, yes. Your son is unwell of the mind. What is his sickness?"

"He gets off to dead things!" The words fell out of Patrick now. "My son is a pervert."

Father Cotton seemed shocked despite being a monster himself. Ironic? Or an indictment of just how sick Brandon was? "Your boy is a necrophiliac?"

Patrick raised an eyebrow. "You had that word in your time?"

"It is Latin, and a perversion older than you might think. Your son fornicates with the dead?"

"Not exactly, but I've found him tugging himself off with... remains. The first time, I found him masturbating over a dead bird he'd shot with my air rifle. He was rubbing it against his fucking cock, using its blood for lube. He was only nine, so I gave him a clip 'round the ear and tried to forget about it—not that you can forget a thing like that. A few years later, he was into women, and I thought the whole thing had been a quirk of growing up."

He took a deep breath before he shared the rest of his confession. "One day I was clearing junk out of the garage and found a scrapbook full of photographs. The pictures were of celebrities—Angelina Jolie and the like."

Father Cotton was frowning, and Patrick realised he was losing the man.

"Celebrities are famous entertainers, known throughout the world. Brandon had drawn all over their pictures, nooses around their throats, maggots in their eyes. The pages were stiff and stained where he'd spunked over them. I threw the scrapbook away and told myself it was normal. Just a young boy finding his sexuality. Then the neighbour's cat went missing. Then their dog."

"Oh dear," said Father Cotton, growing pale.

"The poor mutt was still half alive when I found Brandon fucking it. His dick was covered in shit and blood, and he didn't even know I was there at first. I beat him black and blue—first time I ever laid a hand on him. I'm not a violent man, Father, but I still have nightmares about that evening—about how much I lost it with my boy. We were both in a trance, sick with our own emotions. I wonder if I made Brandon the way he is. Did I do something?"

"The son is not responsible for the sins of the father. Nor is the father of the son's. Do not blame yourself for the Devil's deeds."

"You think my son has the Devil in him?"

Father Cottton sighed. "I used to attribute the Devil to many things, even when I should not have. I am reticent to use his name in a literal sense anymore, but I believe your son may have worms in his mind. Perhaps those worms may be removed. The only way to find out is to reach your son and keep him safe. You have watched over him as best you can, Patrick. God wishes no more from a father than that, but like God's own children, fathers can only control their offspring's actions so much. You are not to blame, Patrick. Perhaps neither is your son."

Patrick realised he had tears in his eyes, and a rush of emotions threatened to floor him. It felt good to share his torment with another, but to receive understanding was more than he could bear. "I have kept my boy as close as I've been able to, but I realise now that I've failed him. He needs proper help—professional treatment. I won't let him die in this place, Father. He has his entire life ahead of him, and he is going to get well."

Father Cotton stood and placed both hands on Patrick's head. "Then you understand what you must do. Leave this church, and put an end to this dark place forever. May the village of Abbeydale finally rest in peace. You are absolved of all your sins, my child."

Patrick hugged the priest and nodded curtly. "Thank you, father. Oh, you know they renamed the village Cottontree, right? Is it named after you?"

Father Cotton's eyes went wide. "I'm sorry, what?"

CHAPTER 13

Thunder boomed, but still it did not rain. Tom looked up at the featureless sky and saw no clouds. He knew, somehow, that it could never rain here. The riverbed was a distortion, like a monkey mimicking a human being. There were certain things of which it was not capable.

"Do you think this is what Hell is like?" he asked Sophie as the two of them searched the house for anything useful. So far, they had found nothing but dry mud and splinters.

"It already is Hell," she replied. "Just not for us. It's Hell for Jonathan and the other villagers who burnt Emily Tanner alive. How could he have done that to his own wife?"

Tom huffed. "And we thought *we* had a screwed-up marriage."

"I know, right? Least you never executed me for witchcraft." She picked up a broom from the corner of the room and examined it. "Do you think the woman we met really was Emily Tanner? I don't know what to believe. She did try to help us, but she also wanted us to go down into the cellar."

Tom wasn't sure either. "She wanted us in that cellar just like Jonathan did. If Emily is innocent, then why would she want to feed us to that thing like he did?"

"Maybe it wasn't Emily."

"Who else could it have been?"

Sophie put the broom back down. "Maybe it was Martha? The

witch who made this place. Maybe Martha was pretending to be Emily."

"But why?"

"To make us trust her. More sacrifices for the toad."

Tom chuckled and then rubbed at his eyes. "Can you believe what's coming out of our mouths? We're talking about sacrifices to a toad."

Sophie saw the funny side too, and they both laughed. The situation was so absurd that it was hard to accept as reality. Even now, after all he'd seen, Tom still felt like he was floating through a dream.

"Don't forget about Brandon," said Sophie. "A flying man took him out of the roof."

"Yeah," Tom replied, smirking. "To fucking Narnia."

"Better than the cellar."

They laughed a little while longer until Tom felt so weak he needed to sit down. He took one of the chairs in the room that had somehow reduced to two when he hadn't been looking. "Remember when we first met? We were both studying at the university, but you kept a job at that fast food chicken place?"

"While you took it easy on your parents' money? Yes, I remember. I hated that job. Most miserable years of my life."

Tom nodded. "I was unhappy too, remember? My sister had just passed away in a car accident, and I was drinking all the time. Every night, I used to come in half-cut to order chicken wings, and every night you would put up with my bullshit."

"I could see you were hurting. Even before the night you had a breakdown, I could see your pain."

Tom nodded. The memories were sore, but comforting too, like a healing wound after surgery. He had missed his sister so much and for so long, that he thought he might die too for a while, yet now she was barely a memory to him. It had been so long. Still, her loss had shaped his life.

"The day I lost the plot, I'd been threatened with expulsion from my degree. My tutors were sick of me not turning up, or being drunk during lectures. My parents were furious too, but they were too wrapped up in their own grief to truly care. I started the evening with an entire bottle of Tequila, and I didn't stop there."

Sophie nodded gravely. "You were plastered with vomit by the time you ended up at my counter. You're lucky I was alone. Anybody else would have called the police."

"But you didn't. You sat me down and fed me, cleaned me up and got me half-sober. We spoke till three in the morning. I helped you close up, and I told you everything. But why did you listen?"

Before she gave an answer, she took the remaining chair and placed it next to his. "Because I was unhappy too. I was working every hour God sent just to afford my rent and studying when I should have been sleeping. I was ready to have my own breakdown. Somehow, being there for you that night gave me strength. It showed me how hard life is for everyone. Your problems took my mind off my own, so I listened to you."

"And the following morning, I took you out for breakfast, and I listened to you in return. I think I was in love with you by the time the bill came."

She smiled, glancing upwards as she reminisced. "Within a week, our miseries had gone, huh? At least it felt like it, despite the problems still being there. We used to see each other two hours a week if we were lucky, but it was enough to make everything else bearable. God, Tom, how long ago was that? Our entire lives hinged on you throwing up on yourself that evening twenty years ago."

That was the point Tom was getting at. "Us being together turned our shitty lives into something wonderful."

"I suppose it did."

He put his hand on top of hers. "If this is Hell, maybe we can make it be okay. If we have each other, things won't be that bad."

"But if this is Hell, Tom, why would we be together? Wouldn't we be alone, or with people who would drive us mad?"

Tom removed his hand from hers, struck by something. "Shit! Maybe you're right. Maybe the last thing you want is being stuck with me for all eternity. I'm sorry."

She grabbed his hand and put it back on hers. "Don't be an idiot. Anyway, you said we were getting out of here."

"I'm just stalling while I wait for inspiration. I already know the answer though—we need to kill the monk."

"That means going outside, doesn't it?"

"Don't worry, Soph. I'll protect you."

She punched him in the arm and went over to the door. "My damsel days are behind me. Let's just get this over with."

They went outside, back into the gloomy dusk that never became night. The bridge overhead was gone, but the burnt oak tree had moved right up against the front door. They had to squeeze around it to get passed. The scent of burning wood filled their nostrils.

"What is with this tree?" Tom said. "Does it mean anything?"

"It's the Hickory Tree," said Sophie, so casually it made Tom feel like he should understand what the hell she was talking about.

"You know this tree? What is it?"

She shrugged. "I learned about it at the abbey, on the same school trip I learned about the river bifurcation. The Hickory Tree was where the villagers in Cottontree passed their punishments. They whipped people against the tree and hanged them from its branches. The tree was anointed by the abbot, and he proclaimed that God would see all who repented in its shadow. When such practises were abolished, the tree was chopped down and used in the construction of an altar for the village church—at least that's what they said."

"Cottontree has quite the history. No wonder you hate it."

"That's not the reason."

Tom looked at her. Sophie had never spoken much about her childhood, and he had never pushed her to, lest a fight ensue. They were both pragmatic forward-thinking people who felt the past was the past. Now, however, it seemed like she needed to address her history, so he gave her the chance to speak about it. "What happened to you here as a kid, Soph?"

She closed her eyes, and tears spilled down her cheeks. "When I was twelve, a fire burned down my school and killed forty-six people. Thirty-seven were children."

"Shit! Why didn't you ever tell me?"

"Because I started the fire."

The ground shook, but Tom realised it was his knees buckling. He put a hand against the burnt oak tree to keep from falling. "You burnt down your school?"

She nodded. It was no joke. What he was hearing was the truth. And there was more. "I was smoking with my friend, Joanne. I hated it, but it was the cool thing to do. We hid where we usually did: inside a little nook between the science building and the assembly-hall fire exit. The school kept their bins there, and it was easy to duck down if a teacher came. It was my cigarette that set fire to the bins. I threw it in there after I thought I'd stubbed it out. When Joanne and I saw the smoke rising out of the bins, we panicked. We ran into the assembly hall just as everyone was going in for lunch and tried to act casual. We never told a soul what was happening outside."

Tom shook his head. "You were just kids."

"But I knew, Tom! I knew I'd done something really bad. I saw the first flickering flames coming out of the bin, and I still ran. When the smoke eventually alerted everyone in the hall, it was already too late. The assembly hall was old, with dilapidated oak around the windows and doors. Part of the roof fell in before anyone even realised there was a fire, and it blocked the fire exit. There was another exit, and everyone rushed to get through it at once, causing a big crush. My former tutor, Mrs Radish, got pinned under the notice board when it got knocked over. I remember her looking me right in the eye as she lay there, trapped in the path of the oncoming fire. I swear she knew it was me. She burned right in front of me."

"God, Soph. Did anyone ever find out?"

She shook her head, staring off into the distance like she saw something. "They knew the fire started in the bins, and they found a pack of cigarettes on Joanne's body."

"Joanne died?"

Sophie nodded, tears like torrents on her cheeks. "She tried to help Mrs Radish. She understood what we'd done. Joanne never left Mrs Radish's side the whole time, not even when the smoke choked her unconscious. I should have helped her, but I stood there, staring, until one of the dinner ladies dragged me out. No one ever knew I had anything to do with the fire."

Tom was silent against the tree. What Sophie had admitted was absurd. No way could he have been married to someone with such a huge secret, and yet he had known her long enough to understand that she was utterly sincere in what she was telling him—his wife had killed dozens of people.

Despite the shock and horror of her admission, it was only her anguish that upset him. Why had she never trusted him enough to share her burden? Did she think he would blame her?

"If every twelve-year-old who did a shitty thing had to pay for it, we'd have no kids left. You were a child, Soph, and the fear of admitting what you did was too much. Did you, for one second, ever intend for anyone to get hurt?"

She shook her head, sobbing. "No."

"Then it was just a tragic accident. Kids smoke, fires start, people die. There's not much sense to the world, and there never has been."

"That's what I used to think, but now I know there's more. There's a place after death, and if I get what I deserve, I will pay for what I did as a child. I'll pay for it, Tom."

Tom wished he were a priest, or a lecturer who could come up with some grand philosophy about life and the ever after, but he wasn't. He was an accountant, and accountants were not the most philosophical of people.

"You were just a child, Soph, and if there is a God, I don't think He would blame a child for making a mistake."

"You really believe that?"

"Come here." He pulled her into a hug. "Thank you for telling me."

"I'm a monster, Tom."

"I've seen monsters, and you're not one of them."

She moved out of his grasp. "You're right. It's this fucking village. Cottontree is evil. This place is cursed, and I will not be stuck here. Fuck this place, Tom. Fuck it."

Her sudden change of mood was jarring, but he considered her anger might be healthier than self-loathing, so he did not stand in her way. "Absolutely, fuck this place."

She wiped snot from her nose and smiled in a grimace. "Fuck this mad house and the monster in the cellar. Fuck blind monks and witches. And FUCK. THIS. UGLY. FUCKING. TREE." She leapt past Tom and grabbed the lowest hanging bough, and like a body builder she chinned herself up until she was using all of her weight to try to drag the wretched thing down.

The branch snapped with an echo off the embankments on either side. Sophie splatted on the ground, landing on her back and moaning. A thick length of blackened wood rested in her arms, and she clutched it like a baby against her chest.

The dead tree came to life. Its broken limb bled foul black mud, and its trunk thrashed like a floundering elk. The wind picked up and billowed around them. Tom grabbed Sophie and pulled her to her feet, trying to get her away from whatever was happening. "I think you pissed it off, Soph!"

Sophie brandished the detached limb in front of her. "Good. Fuck you, tree!"

"Another thing I never thought one of us would ever say. Time to leave?"

The tree stopped moving.

"I... I think it's okay," said Sophie. "See... nothing to worry about."

A woman stepped out from behind the tree, fingering its broken stump like a concerned mother. She wore an old-timey dress like the last woman they had met, but hers was ivory, not green. She was also much shorter than the woman who claimed to be Emily Tanner. At first, the woman acted like she hadn't noticed the two of them standing there, but then she glanced at them curiously. "You damaged my tree?"

"Sorry," said Tom quickly. "We were just... sorry."

Just when he felt sure the woman would turn into a monster and eat them, she threw herself down on the mud and hugged Tom's knees. "Thank you, sir. Thank you, thank you, thank you! For so long I have been trapped inside this tree. I feared I would forget myself."

"And who are you?" Sophie asked, sounding a little peeved. Tom looked at her and raised an eyebrow. Was she jealous? Probably just at the end of her tether with overdramatic strangers.

"My name is Emily Tanner, and I must warn you—this place is cursed by a great evil."

Sophie huffed. "Thanks, we already know that. How do we get out?"

"You must stop him."

"The monk?"

"Yes! The evil one. The corrupter." The woman winced as if her head hurt. "It has been so long. I... I feel something coming. Something bad. You must... you must fight the monk!"

Tom saw bones rise up out of the ground. Instinctively, he pulled Sophie close to him. She was still clutching the tree limb—it was sharp and resembled a short spear. The rattling of chains echoed off the riverbanks.

Tom took the tree branch from Sophie and held it in both hands. It looked like a spear, so he would use it as one.

"Looks like it's time for church."

ॐ

PATRICK WOKE UP IN THE MUD ALONGSIDE MIA AND GWEN. His memory was a blur, but not like last time because things quickly came back to him. He remembered Father Cotton placing his hands on his head and reciting strange verses from the bible. He remembered getting sleepy, but before he fell asleep, he had seen a flash of panic on the priest's face, as if suddenly he had remembered he'd left an oven on somewhere. Then blackness had consumed Patrick, and he was waking up in the mud again.

It was getting old.

He and the girls knew what they were supposed to do—find the house beneath the bridge and fight the toad. Then its acolytes, Jonathan and Martha, would come running. By killing the demon's carers, they could cut off its food supply and leave it forever weakened and trapped in this place. Martha's spell would also be broken, allowing the innocent to leave.

Whether that included Patrick, he didn't know.

"Which way should we go?" Mia asked him. She clutched her ridiculously long hair in her hands and wrung it like wet washing.

Patrick got up off the ground and looked in both directions; he saw only mud. "I'm not sure it matters, luv. This bloody place takes you where it pleases. Let's just pick a direction and hope for the best. I need to find Brandon."

"We will," said Gwen. "Everything will work out. Just need to go kick a toad in the nuts first."

Patrick laughed. He liked Gwen. Kind of girl he wished Brandon was into—instead of what he really was. "Would you like to do the kicking?"

"We'll see how things pan out. Maybe Mia can use her hair to strangle it."

He looked at the other girl, still wringing her hair.

"Yeah, you really should get that cut, luv. It's a hazard. What if you passed by some working machinery?"

Mia studied the hair bunched in her hands and seemed lost in thought for a moment. When she looked up, there was a determined look on her face. "My dad always said I had beautiful hair, and I suppose that's why I never wanted to cut it. He died when I was nine. Time to let go. First thing I'll do when we get out of here is go get a pair of sharp scissors."

Gwen smiled like it was the best thing she had ever heard. She gave her friend a hug, but then said, "Just a trim. Don't go crazy."

Mia smacked Gwen's rump. "All this time nagging me, and now you're worried I'll cut off too much!"

"You're right. Take it all off, right down to the scalp." Gwen made the motion of a razer going over her head, and they set off down the riverbed, laughing and joking all the way. Patrick felt good too, and wondered if it was because he had become quite sure he would die, or end up in whatever state counted for dead in this place. Was that what had happened to Brandon? Was his son still here somewhere? Or had he gone on to yet another place?

Gwen and Mia held hands as they walked beside Patrick. He suppressed the urge to make some seedy comment as he might have done in the past. He felt like a different man for some reason. Perhaps he truly had unburdened himself back at the church. He was clean and didn't want to dirty himself with the behaviour he might have approved of before. Besides, the two girls' affection was likely little more than comfort, and if his wife were here, he'd be holding her too. That was the first thing he was going to do if he ever got to see her again. He would hold her and tell her he was sorry for not being a better man.

But first, he had to find his son and start being a better father.

"I think I see something," said Mia, pointing up ahead.

Patrick saw it too. "You ladies ready for this?"

They both nodded and let go of each other's hand. The three of them walked faster, not wanting to tire themselves in the thick mud but too eager to take it slower. As they progressed, Patrick could make out people in the distance. "That's Tom and Sophie," he said excitedly. "What are they doing?"

"Oh no," said Gwen. "They're attacking Father Cotton."

"But he's on our side," said Mia.

Patrick shook his head in despair. "They don't know that. Come on! If they kill him, there'll be hell to pay."

༒

Tom quick-stepped towards the blind monk and swung the blackened tree branch like a baseball bat. The monster swatted the blow aside easily, and the branch tumbled into the mud. Tom caught the cuff of his jeans on a ribcage and stumbled, but he was back on his feet instantly, dodging aside just in time to avoid a slicing whip of the monk's chains. Bits of flesh flicked free of the links and spattered his face.

"It must be killed," Emily cried hysterically from beside the house. "It must be killed so this damnation may end."

"Be careful, Tom," Sophie warned.

Tom knelt down and picked up what he thought was a human thigh bone—thick and heavy. Again, he swung it like a baseball bat, except this time he faked sideways then adjusted his grip and delivered an upswing. The bone struck the monster beneath its chin and knocked loose a swatch of oozing flesh. It made no sound, but it stumbled backwards.

He hurt the monster.

Somehow, Tom, a soon-to-be divorced accountant had hurt a creature from Hell. Buoyed by the victory, he swung the thigh bone again, and this time cracked the monk on top of its head. The femur snapped in two, and the monk rocked backwards in the mud, chains flailing around it.

Tom was unarmed. He bent down to grab another bone, but there was nothing the size and weight of the femur. He saw the ribcage that had tripped him and thought he could snap off a rib and use it as a knife. Heart pounding, he raced through the mud towards it.

He stopped six inches short.

His neck squeezed tight as a bloodied chain tightened around it. Panicked, he tried to run, but another chain whipped out and entangled his legs. The pressure on his neck increased. His head was going to pop up into the air like pus from a pimple. The chain at his legs yanked and dropped him onto his knees.

He tried to breathe, but couldn't. His temples pounded.

A familiar face raced towards him—Patrick, accompanied by two young girls. He was shouting something at the top of his lungs, but all Tom could hear was the pulsing blood in his ears. Nothing could save him now—nothing could unwrap the thick chain from around his throat.

Sophie appeared. She retrieved the blackened tree branch from the mud and faced off against the monk. Tom tried to wave her away.

"Go! Get out of here. It's too late for me."

But she was determined. Her eyes locked with the monstrosity's, and she raised the branch over her shoulder like a spear. She had a look of fury on her face as she rammed it into the monk's exposed ribcage.

The monk broke its silence and let out a scream.

Patrick arrived and started fretting, with both hands on his balding head and a look of horror on his face.

Tom still struggled for breath, even as the monk collapsed onto its knees. His vision flickered with lights and spots, and darkness began spreading inwards from his peripheral vision. It had been more than a minute since his last breath, but oxygen flooded into him and he was inhaling with ease. He grabbed for his throat and realised the chain was gone—not just removed, but no longer in existence.

The monk had both hands wrapped around the tree branch jutting out from its ribcage. Flesh dripped from its face and pooled in the mud. The branch began to glow red as if burning in a fire. Then the monk burst into flames.

Tom's vision was still spotty from oxygen deprivation, which made it hard to get up, so he remained there in the mud, slumped over and watching. Before his very eyes, the monk disappeared in the flames until, gradually, the fire died down. Where the monk had been, an elderly man now lay in its place—a priest in drab robes—that was so horribly burned, it was clear the monster had been him. The blind monk was a man. But who was the man?

"No! No! No!" Patrick ran over to the injured priest and cradled him in his arms. He glared at Sophie and cursed at her. "You idiot! What have you done?"

Sophie stood in the mud, confused. "I... I killed a monster."

"He was no monster," said one of the girls, a small blonde who also looked horrified.

"She did what needed to be done," said Emily, walking into the middle of them confidently. She studied the suffering priest with an expression of satisfaction. "Hello, Father Cotton. It's so good to see you again after all these years."

The priest coughed weakly, trying to find his voice. "Emily, is that you?"

Emily took the final steps towards him. The bones sank back down beneath the mud, which was hardening. "Yes, Father. It is me, the woman you burnt to death."

"Forgive me."

Emily smirked. "Never. You delayed my Lord's plans for half-a-millennia. For that, you shall burn here for all eternity as I have since the night you cursed me."

Tom was utterly confused, but he saw the absolute fear and horror in the dying priest's eyes as they seemed to realise something. "You speak of the Lord? The Lord forgives, child."

Emily laughed.

Patrick clutched the priest in his arms and glared up at her warily like a dog guarding a bone.

"I'm not talking about your Lord, priest. My Lord is glorious and rewards those loyal to him. What has your worthless God ever done for you?"

Tom stepped in. "Emily, what are you—"

"Silence!" She threw out a hand and knocked him down with a blast of hot air. Fiery embers burst from her fingertips, which she returned to her sides as she turned back to the priest.

"Burning me alive was part of the plan, you fool. My agony—my life—was to be the final sacrifice to Chordaxis. My ascension would have placed me at his side, to become his wife and instrument. You and the abbot put a stop to that with your pathetic prayers. You cursed me, Father Cotton. Man of God!" She spat at him. "Ha! You didn't even know what you were asking for."

Father Cotton sucked at the air as if trying to catch words with his lips. "I... I don't understand. You are innocent. Martha and Tom..."

"Are my faithful servants. It was all a charade to have you judge and execute an innocent woman—to make me a martyr like your beloved Jesus. I never killed those children with my own hands. Martha slaughtered her own twins and ensured you executed me for it. All part of the plan." She spat again. "You and your monks created this place, Father. You bound a spell in your own dying misery at the steps of the abbey. Now your misery has ended, and my bars are broken. Enjoy your new eternity, for it shall be vile and full of agonies."

She lifted a hand, sharp fingernails fizzing with purple and red flames. Whatever Emily was about to do, she had not the chance, for Patrick dropped the priest and launched himself at her. She was taken by surprise, and he managed to land a vicious head butt right in the centre of her face. She cried out in shock and anger and clutched her nose which was now bleeding. Patrick moved to attack her again, but she put up a hand to stop him.

"You shall pay for that," she snarled, but then, instead of retaliating, she exploded into a mist of fiery embers.

Tom, Sophie, and the others shielded their faces as burning flecks scattered over them, but eventually the heat moved away—towards the house beneath the bridge. It had relocated twenty yards further down the riverbed, and there was now a tilting chimney stack. The mist of embers disappeared down the funnel.

Tom didn't understand what had happened. The only man who might know was the priest, but 'Father Cotton,' as he seemed to be called, was fading fast. He seemed to realise this himself because the priest lifted a burned hand to summon them all closer.

It appeared he had something to say.

CHAPTER 14

Patrick placed himself underneath Father Cotton and held him. Tom sensed a change in the builder and wondered what connection there was between him and the priest. The two girls had introduced themselves as Gwen and Mia, and they along with Stacey had been in the third car on the bridge. That was all Tom had learned so far. Father Cotton did not have long to say what he needed to.

"All these centuries, I have been wrong," he said, seeming a little amused by his own folly, but the distant stare in his eyes was one of devastation. "I thought Emily Tanner was innocent—the only soul to have escaped this place—but I was wrong. She is the great evil that led the downfall of Abbeydale. After we burnt her at the stake and her curse fell upon the village, I crawled back to the abbey, blind and dying. There I told the abbot what I had seen. I begged for his forgiveness, and he gave it, glad to see me crestfallen and ready to accept the Lord's compassion. He carried me into the chancel and assembled the monks there. Together we prayed to God to forgive Abbeydale and prevent Chordaxis's evil from spreading further. Emily's curse brought us here, an offering to their vile lord Chordaxis. But the true Lord met their spell in kind —casting down the evil alongside us and keeping it at bay inside the house beneath the bridge. For centuries, I thought Martha and Jonathan were responsible for it all, and I had put an innocent woman to death. I have tortured myself for so long about this. Perhaps I shall depart to a worse place, but now, at least, I can finally forgive myself."

Patrick stroked the priest's frazzled hair while the two young girls wept. Tom and Sophie glanced at one another and tried to wrap their heads around what they were hearing.

Father Cotton continued, but his voice was fading. His eyes rolled loosely in the spaces between his burnt flesh. "The prayers of the abbey were placed into me as I passed on, tethering this place to my soul. They must have renamed the village in my honour—an undeserved gesture. Jonathan and Martha must have wished my death for hundreds of years, but the curse has kept us separate." He looked at Sophie. "You have inadvertently done their bidding."

Sophie looked offended. "You were a monster. The blind monk."

"An affliction, my child, and not one I could help. I forgive you—you couldn't have known—but the world is now in great peril. Emily and her minions must not be allowed to liberate Chordaxis from his cell. The Great Toad must remain in prison. You must eliminate its handlers."

"You want us to kill Emily and her partners?" said Tom. "How do I know you're telling the truth. How do I—"

"Because he saved me and the girls," Patrick shouted. "While Emily slapped you down with magic and turned into a bunch of fireflies. Do the math."

"But you were a monster," said Sophie, shaking her head as she looked at Father Cotton. She didn't seem like she could make sense of it.

Father Cotton coughed and had to catch his breath before speaking again. "E-Emily focused her curse on me... corrupted my flesh. She is responsible for far worse... crimes than I... Please, trust what your... hearts are..."

Patrick eased the priest onto his back and shushed him. "Enough now, Father. We know what we have to do. Can I help ease your suffering?"

The priest shook his head. "No, my child. Allow me to enjoy the pain a while longer. Once I am gone, the spell shall be broken and Chordaxis will be stronger than ever. Go, while there is still time."

"Where?" Sophie asked.

"Into... the... house. Go!"

Patrick placed the priest to rest on the hardening mud and stood up. "Safe travels, Father. And thank you."

Father Cotton was too weak to reply, so they left him lying on the ground staring up at the sky. Patrick glanced back several times, but no one else did. Tom found himself at the front of the pack, and he stopped in front of the house. Whilst they had been distracted, the small wooden door had turned into a ten-foot arch-way, barred by a thick iron door. There was no knocker, which seemed like a deliberate omission.

"It's changed again," said Sophie. "I can't see the bridge either."

"What do you mean?" Patrick asked. Tom frowned. Of course, the builder had not yet seen this wretched place.

"This house has trouble being one thing or the other," Tom explained. "It doesn't matter... Are we going in or not?"

No one hesitated. Tom pushed on the iron door, and it swung open easily.

An endless hallway met them.

"This is new," said Sophie.

The hallway was cut from smooth grey stone like a tunnel eroded through rock. It shone with a fine layer of moisture and echoed each time a drip sounded. Were they in the deep belly of a lair, due to encounter a monster within? Tom no longer cared. What worse was there to come? Death? So be it.

"So, Emily was the big bad this whole time," said Gwen. "How did Father Cotton not know?"

"Because she was trapped in a tree," said Sophie. "Until I let her out. The legends come back to me now. My sister used to try and scare me as a child by telling me there was an old tree—the Hickory Tree—that would grow in your garden at night, and if you got up too early and looked out your bedroom window, the Devil's wife would look back at you and drag you down beneath its roots. How did I ever forget that stupid story? My sister was such a bitch."

"Sounds like she was right though," said Patrick.

Sophie grimaced. "I suppose she was."

Gwen grunted. "So you let Emily out and killed Father Cotton. Good job, Hero."

Sophie looked like she might slap the girl, so Tom reached out and touched her arm. "No one is to blame here," he said. "Except, maybe Brandon."

"What about my son?" Patrick asked eagerly. He had been leaning against the stone wall breathing heavily, but now he pushed himself away and stood tall. "What happened to him?"

"Jonathan took him," Tom clenched his fists, "right after he told me how he caused the crash that landed us all here."

"What? Don't talk bollocks. I was the one driving, so how could Brandon have caused the accident?"

Tom glared at Patrick. "Because he didn't tie down your tools, you fucking moron."

Patrick sneered and took a step closer. "You sure you want to make an enemy of me, you stuck-up prick? I'll wipe the floor with you."

Sophie stood between the two of them. She pointed a finger in Patrick's face. "Touch my husband and I'll do to you what I did to your goddamn priest!"

"And then you'll have me and Gwen to deal with," said Mia. "I'll stamp your head in my—"

"Hold on a minute," Tom shouted, and his voice echoed off down the tunnel. "Everybody stop!"

Everyone froze and looked at him. Tom felt like he might burst an artery, so much pressure in his skull—a swarm of flies in his head.

Fireflies.

"Why are we at each other's throats?" he asked them as calmly as he could, even though he wanted to throttle them all.

"Because you and your missus screwed everything up," said Patrick, his fists clenched, and his jaw jutting out.

Tom kept his palms up while he talked, trying to prevent a fight. "We're all stuck here together. We're on the same side. Patrick? Brandon was alive when we last saw him, okay, but Jonathan took him. He was fighting right beside us, and we will all help you find him."

Patrick still looked angry, but he could find no reason to argue, so instead, he nodded. "Thank you."

"This place is making us angry," said Gwen, seeming to realise what Tom had. "This tunnel is affecting us—it's wrong."

Mia jolted as if the same realisation suddenly hit her too. "It's Emily. Her influence."

Patrick was the last to back down, but once he did, he did so completely. He looked embarrassed as he spoke to Tom. "I'm so sorry, mate."

"It's okay, Patrick. We have to remember we're in this together. I don't understand all that's gone on with you three, and believe me, you don't know what Sophie and I have been through either— but we were all fucked the moment we drove onto that bridge. Let's find a way to un-fuck ourselves."

Everyone took a moment to calm themselves, and Tom felt the fireflies leave his skull. Whatever tricks Emily was capable of, he wouldn't make it easy for her.

As if to taunt them, the sound of a woman's cackling echoed off the stone walls.

"Think that was an invitation?" said Gwen.

Tom looked down the tunnel but saw nothing. "Stay close together. Be ready for anything. Let's go."

Not wanting to lose his determination, Tom started jogging, leading the others—a pack of marooned strangers who didn't know each other well enough to trust one another—deeper into the tunnel. It was only their shared suffering that united them.

They huffed and puffed as they jogged—especially Patrick— and they went on that way until Tom started to suspect the corridor went on forever. Then, just when he was almost out of breath, it succumbed to reality, and a light flickered up ahead. It came from a torch, like the one Tom had used against the creature in the cellar.

When they reached it, they saw that it illuminated the entrance to a spiral staircase cut into the stone. Staring down the gap was like peering into the bowels of a snake, and Tom had to glance at his companions to check their resolve.

Once they nodded, Tom took the first step downwards. "No going back now."

No sound existed in the stairwell aside from the drip-drip of the moisture seeping from the walls. The descent took them an age, but unlike the tunnel, it always felt like they were making progress. Sure enough, they eventually emerged into a room at the bottom of the stairs.

The stench was disabling.

A thousand corpses decorated the room.

"I'm going to be sick," said Mia, who kept her word and vomited off to the side.

"What is this place?" asked Gwen. She glanced around with both hands glued to her horrified cheeks. Strung to the wall beside her was a naked, headless torso with huge breasts. A road map of cuts and slices crisscrossed her body, and a pile of assorted limbs filled a basket at her feet. The entire wall was lined with corpses, many of them dismembered or pierced by an assortment of twisted instruments and tools.

Tom staggered and almost put his hand against a line of dangling eyeballs before realising—the vile item resembled a string of garlic cloves.

In the centre of the room, lit by torches on poles, lay a dead woman with long, bloodstained blonde hair. Her slender body drooped forwards over a wooden wedge mounted on legs so that her exposed rear pointed up into the air.

Gwen repeated her earlier question. "What is this place?"

"It is the resting place of the damned," came a voice. "This is what remains of the population of Abbeydale."

A shadow moved in the corner from where the voice came. The tone was familiar, but Tom could not yet be certain of its owner.

"Who's there?"

A creature emerged, entering the firelight of the room's torches. It stared at them from behind the face of a woman—a face skinned and removed before being fashioned into a mask. Tom realised, with dread, that the face had once belonged to Stacey.

Mia puked again.

Gwen howled.

Yet it was Patrick who was most shocked. "B-Brandon, is that you?"

The creature raised its arms in a mockery of Christ on the

cross. It wore a suit of human flesh that swished with even the tiniest of movements. "Brandon was a name given to a single body," it said. "I am Many. We are many. We are the dead."

The creature snatched the tangled hair of the dead girl mounted on the wedge and pulled her head up. The corpse had no face, and must have been Stacey. "Behold, what is mine. All that is dead."

"You always were a weirdo," said Mia angrily, wiping her puke-stained mouth.

Gwen grabbed an instrument that had been clamped around the genitals of a male corpse hanging from the wall and tore it loose. "I'm going to fucking kill you."

Patrick stood in front of her. "Stay back! That's my son."

The creature calling itself 'Many' fidgeted behind Stacey's corpse, pulling aside a flap in his flesh-suit. An erect penis slipped out. "My master gave their remains to me," he said gleefully—like a child on Christmas morning. "They all belong to me."

"Get away from her," Gwen screamed.

Ignoring her, the creature slid its penis into Stacey's corpse and moaned with ecstasy. "This is paradise," it said, "and you shall not take it from me."

Tom was at a loss, so he stared at Patrick. "What the fuck is with your son, Patrick?"

Patrick stared back vacantly. His breathing was heavy, and he wobbled back and forth. "B-B-Brandon has a few... a few issues. My son just needs help, that's all."

"I'm going to cut his fucking dick off," said Gwen, opening and shutting the instrument she held in her hands. They were like a nightmarish version of bolt cutters, and testicle sinew still hung from their blades.

Gwen moved towards Brandon, but Patrick stood in her way. "You take one more step and I'll add you to the walls, girl."

Tom pulled Gwen back out of harm's way, but couldn't understand what he was hearing. "Patrick, what the fuck are you doing? Your son has gone to the dark side."

In the background, Brandon thrusted away at Stacey's corpse. Her head flopped up and down with every violating prod.

"He went there a long time ago," said Mia. "I know a girl who said they saw him in the school bathroom sticking dead flies down the end of his dick. I never believed it 'til now."

Patrick roared, "IT'S JUST A PHASE!"

Tom stepped back. Patrick was the biggest guy in the room and enraged like a bull. "Okay, Patrick. No one is going to make a move. This is your call, but right now, your son is wearing a young girl's face and sticking his dick in her corpse. I don't want to teach you how to parent, but—"

"Do you have kids?" Patrick snapped. "Oh no, that's right, you and your wife never did. So, is it you firing blanks? Or is your bitch barren?" Sophie winced, and Patrick spotted her reaction. He grinned. "Ah, so you're the one with defective parts. It's a wonder he stuck around, luv."

Sophie closed her eyes and turned away. "Let's fucking leave him here with his sicko son."

Tom put his hands up peacefully. "Patrick. We need you to keep the figures in front of you. We can leave your son here and deal with him later, but we have important things to do first."

Patrick shook his head, tears on his rough cheeks. "I'm not losing him again. I-I need to take care of him."

Gwen moved again with the testicle remover, and this time Patrick lashed out and grabbed her by the throat. Tom didn't want to escalate the situation, so he stood where he was.

"Patrick? Patrick listen to me. I already said this is your call. Let go of Gwen, and we will deal with this however you want, but we can't turn on each other, okay?"

Patrick glanced sideways at Tom before pushing Gwen away. She rubbed her neck and glared at him, but she backed off because she had lost the testicle remover to him. He brandished it at her now. "Stay back, all of you! Let me talk to my boy."

Brandon was still pumping away at Stacey's corpse, unconcerned with any of the living. Patrick stepped closer to him and put a hand on his chest. "Bran, listen to me, son. You need to stop what you are doing. You need help. I will get you better, okay?" Brandon seemed not to hear, so Patrick pushed more firmly. "Boy, I just gave you an order."

Brandon flinched behind his flesh mask, eyes focusing on his father. With a disgusting *plop*, he stepped backwards. His throbbing penis dripped with blood and gore. Mia threw up again in the corner, but Patrick placed his hands on his son's shoulders lovingly.

"Good lad, Brandon. This place isn't real. It's evil. I don't want you to be evil, Brandon. Bran, do you hear me?"

Brandon nodded. "I don't want to hide any more, dad. I don't want to keep fighting to be something I'm not."

"I understand, Bran, but you're sick. Let me help you."

"No! No, I'm not sick." Brandon's face screwed up in a grimace, and he hissed. He shoved Patrick backwards and sent him sprawling against Stacey's corpse, which slid from its perch and crumpled on the floor. Gwen and Mia rushed forward to retrieve their friend's body.

Brandon grabbed a metal spike out of a body on the floor and pointed it at his father. "Here, I can be who I want to be."

Patrick trembled, the testicle remover in his hand dangling back and forth.

"Son, listen to me. Let's get out of here, and we can talk things through. Jonathan, Emily, Martha... they are all evil! They are all fucking evil. You want to be damned alongside them, stuck in this place for eternity?"

Brandon looked around the room, at the tapestry of filth and flesh lining the walls. "This place isn't Hell. It is Heaven. You won't take me away from here; I won't let you!"

Brandon lunged at his father and planted the metal spike in the space between his collar bone and neck. Patrick grunted and swore, but he didn't let the attack drop him. Instead, he shoved his much lighter son and sent him hurtling away. Brandon bounced off a hanging corpse, stunned, but then resumed his attack. This time, he had no weapon, for the spike still jutted from Patrick's neck.

Tom cried out. "Patrick, be careful!"

"Just stay back," he shouted. "Stay away from my boy."

Sophie and Tom exchanged worried glances.

Brandon panted like a lusting animal. His erect penis still jutted from his flesh costume. He reached down and grabbed a wicked-looking knife, short and curved—most likely used for skinning poor victims alive. Now he tried using it on his own father. Patrick grappled with him, trying to keep the deadly blade at bay. They dodged back and forth in a desperate Waltz.

Tom had seen enough. He rushed to help Patrick.

"Get back," Patrick shouted. He kicked out and struck Tom in the knee. Tom doubled over in pain.

Brandon slipped his father's grasp and drove the knife into the side of his arm. Patrick growled in agony as blood spurted along his forearm and dripped from his fingertips.

Sophie screamed at the top of her lungs. "Brandon, stop! He's your dad!"

Brandon didn't listen. He yanked the knife out of Patrick's neck and used it to slice open his stomach. Foul black blood bloomed on his shirt.

"You're going to kill him," Tom shouted.

Brandon snarled, a wild animal, and lifted the blade to deliver the killing blow. But Patrick found strength and grabbed his son's face.

Surprised, Brandon lashed out and buried the knife in his father's ribs, but Patrick did not let go. He pressed his thumbs into the eyeholes of his son's mask.

Brandon wailed, a tortured spirit, and fought free of his father's probing—but the damage had been done. He cupped his face in his hands and dropped to his knees.

Patrick did the same, blood gushing from multiple wounds and staining the ground.

Tom wanted to help, but Patrick waved him away. "Leave us. Leave me with... my boy."

Brandon removed his hands from his face and revealed two bleeding holes where his eyes had been. Patrick had blinded his son.

"Come here, boy," said Patrick, reaching out. "Let me hold you."

No fight left in him, Brandon slumped against his father and allowed himself to be embraced. The two of them hugged tightly, like any normal father and son.

"I will never leave this place, dad. I belong here. Listen to me, please."

Patrick rubbed his son's back lovingly. Their blood poured in rivers from their bodies and mingled on the floor. "I am listening, son. I'm sorry I didn't before. This is where you will be happy, I see that now. No one will judge you here."

Brandon sobbed. "I can stay? Really?"

"Yes, son. I love you."

At first, Tom didn't realise what was happening. Father and son were silent, still embracing, but then Brandon began to claw at his father's back. Grunts and panicked exhaling came from them both.

Sophie and Tom exchanged more worried glances.

Brandon's clawing turned to beating as he batted his fists frantically against his father's back, but Patrick held onto his son tightly, squeezing him harder—crushing him. Tom realised Patrick had one of his meaty hands wrapped around his son's windpipe, whilst keeping him trapped with his other thick arm.

The boy was half the size of his father, and the blood-slick floor made it too hard to gain purchase. His naked feet slid back and forth on the wet stone floor.

Tom took a step, but Sophie grabbed his arm and shook her head. He sighed and stepped back again.

He was letting this happen.

It ended quickly. Brandon's struggling increased tempo for a few seconds, reaching a crescendo, but then stopped suddenly as if a switch had been flipped.

Father and son went still.

Tom moved again. "Patrick, why don't you come over to us." Patrick did not move. He remained on his knees, cradling his son against his chest. Tom took another step but waited, not wanting to alert the father who had just killed his son. "Patrick?"

Still, Patrick did not move. Tom had no choice but to continue. What Patrick had done was tragic, yet Tom didn't blame the man. His son was sick beyond repair, and it was a kindness killing him to keep him from spending eternity in this place. Was that how it worked? Was Brandon someplace else now?

"Patrick, please answer me. Are you okay?"

Now Tom became concerned. Patrick did not move a muscle. He didn't even sob for his child. It didn't even look like he was breathing.

Tom took the last couple of steps and positioned himself so he could see Patrick's face. The man's cheeks were ghostly pale, and his eyes were closed. Blood pooled, an inch thick, at his knees.

Patrick was dead—murdered son in his arms.

Tom shook his head at Sophie and groaned. "He's gone. Too much blood."

"Oh no," said Mia. "Poor Patrick."

Gwen folded her arms and looked stricken. "He was all right."

Sophie rubbed at her neck. She had taken to performing the gesture as if it were some kind of comfort. "What a horrible thing to have to do. This place... this fucking place."

Tom knew how she felt. All of them had crested fear. Now all they felt was anger. Perhaps it was Emily's influence, but Tom wanted to smash this place apart with his bare hands. He looked around at the gore and bodies hanging from the walls.

"Let's get out of this place."

Gwen eased Stacey's mutilated corpse onto the ground and placed her arms over her breasts. Then she retrieved the testicle slicer and stood up.

"Let's go find the bastards responsible for our worst day ever."

ত৩৩

THE NEXT ROOM WAS A TWISTED VERSION OF A CHURCH. THE pews were cut from bone, and a giant crucifix at the far end of the nave hung upside down, with an image of Jesus hanging by the ankles. Stain-glassed windows created blood red shafts of light.

Martha and Jonathan knelt at the front before a bone altar.

The two monsters were yet to realise Tom and the others had entered behind them, which was why Sophie grabbed Tom and pulled him behind the rear-most pews. Gwen and Mia took notice and did the same.

"This is Father Cotton's church," whispered Gwen. "It's all twisted, but it's the same, I know it."

Tom frowned. "Okay. What does that mean?"

"I don't know. Father Cotton said his church was a sanctuary created by God. If this is it, it no longer has anything to do with God."

"The spell is broken," said Mia. "The monk's spell created the church when they asked for God's protection. Now it's twisted like everything else."

"Then we don't have much time." Tom peeked over the top of the pews to ensure they were still undetected. Jonathan and Martha were still kneeling before the altar. "We need to put an end to this right now."

Sophie grunted. "How? What should we do, rush them?"

Gwen scissored her testicle slicer. "Sounds good to me."

"We have to think about this," said Mia. "They took Brandon and messed with his mind. They could have killed him, but instead, they recruited him. Perhaps one of us should stumble out and act like we want to be on their side."

"Really?" said Sophie. "That's your idea? It's stupid."

Mia shrugged, bunching her dark hair together and throwing it behind her shoulder. "I'll do it. Time to grow up."

"Mia," said Gwen. "Don't be an idiot."

"I'm not an idiot, Gwen. I'll distract them while you guys creep around the pews and ambush them." She nodded at Gwen's testicle slicer. "You'll finally get your chance to use that thing."

Gwen appeared happy at the prospect, and Tom decided he was a little glad he'd never had children. Sophie, however, seemed impressed by Mia's plan.

"If you pretend to be desperate," she said. "They might hesitate about killing you. Buy us one minute and we can come up behind them."

"What do we do then?" asked Gwen. "Can we even hurt them?"

Tom pictured Brandon stabbing Jonathan with his own sword and nodded. "We can do our best, that much I promise you."

"So, we have a plan," said Gwen, "but there's one thing we're missing."

Sophie frowned. "What?"

"Emily! She's the Cruella in charge, so, where is she?"

"I'm sure we'll find out," said Sophie. "Let's settle one account at a time."

They waited on Mia while she summoned whatever strength she needed. Then, without a word, she stepped into the aisle and started waving her arms.

CHAPTER 15

"I give up," said Mia in a voice sounding realistically terrified. "Please, just let me out of this place. Please!"

Sophie kept her head down and so did the others. They couldn't risk being spotted now that Mia was in danger. She was insane for doing this, but Sophie respected the girl for refusing to play the damsel in distress. Gwen didn't shy away either by the looks of her. That one was a fighter.

From their hiding spots, they couldn't see what was going on. It left them no choice but to wait and listen.

Martha spoke first. "Ah, one of the young ladies. Are you looking for your friends? I believe we left one of them in the care of Brandon. What a revelation that boy turned out to be."

Jonathan chuckled. "As dark hearted as they come, that one. And there was me planning to torture him and be done. What a waste that would have been."

"I-I haven't seen Brandon," said Mia. "I was with Gwen, b-b-but she left me. I was... I was scared, and that bitch fucking left me. If I find her, I'll tear her goddamn eyes out."

Her comments elicited silence, and Sophie imagined the confused expressions on Martha and Jonathan's faces.

"Do you understand what we are, girl?" Martha asked. "I suggest you run."

"I know what you are," said Mia. "Father Cotton said you're witches."

"Actually, I am a warlock," Jonathan corrected, "but you're close enough. Let me tell you something about witches and warlocks, little sparrow. We simply love to sacrifice juicy little virgins, like you."

"I... I'm not a virgin. I've had sex."

Martha cackled, but then fell to silence. "Oh, she's actually speaking the truth. I can smell it on her. So, come on, my sweet, who was the lucky gentleman? Your daddy or your uncle?"

"My best friend's brother."

Gwen shifted behind the pew. "Does she mean my brother? I'll wring her bloody neck."

Mia continued. "I was staying over at my friend Gwen's house one night, and I snuck into her brother's room. I don't know what possessed me—I've fancied him for ages. I didn't say a word as I got into bed with him. We screwed, and I left, but the next morning he wouldn't even look at me. It was so humiliating. I've wanted to tell Gwen for a while. If only so I can rub it in her perfect, smug, little face. She thinks she's so amazing with the car her daddy bought her and her perfect fucking life. Well, I fucked her brother, so the joke's on her."

Gwen was fuming behind the pews, biting her lip and snarling. Sophie reached out to keep her from exploding. "She's playing a part, sweetie."

Gwen seemed not to hear her.

"Come on," Tom whispered. "We need to get moving."

As one, they formed a line and crept around the side of the pews. Meanwhile, Mia's strategy continued to play out.

"Why are you still standing here, little girl?" Martha asked. "Are you going to insist we disembowel you? Okay then, so be it."

Mia screamed.

Sophie saw Tom was about to leap up and do something, and she had to stop him. He was always so brash. Couldn't he ever wait to see how the numbers added up before acting?

Despite her screams, Mia was still on task. "Help me teach her a lesson. Help me fuck the bitch up once and for all. That's what you do, right? You wreck people? You destroy your enemies. I want to be like you."

Martha cackled. "Oh, don't we just, little sparrow. We used to bring entire communities to their knees."

"Until Father Cotton messed it all up," said Mia. "This was his church. He didn't even know he was responsible for you being trapped here. He thought it was Emily who cast the spell, not the monks."

Sophie winced. It sounded like Mia was criticising them. Not a good plan.

Martha growled. "Careful, girl. You're tempting me to drag your death out."

"No, please," said Mia. "I just meant that religious idiots meddled with your plans. I get it. My parents are Muslims."

Jonathan spat. "Animals from a distant continent."

"But the same brand of bullshit, I promise you," said Mia. "I hate it. I hate Gwen, religion, my parents... my entire fucking life."

"Then it is a good thing I am about to end it," said Martha.

"Let me join you! Teach me! I want to be a witch. I want to make my enemies tremble and destroy all of God's churches."

Sophie froze, and so did the others. This was the crux of Mia's plan, and all repercussions would hinge upon its outcome. They had only made it halfway around the pews by now, and if Martha didn't go for what Mia was offering, they wouldn't have time to leap out and save her.

"Why should we waste our time with you, girl?" Jonathan spoke in a voice that did not sound amenable to the idea of having an apprentice.

"Because I am young, and your master would want new recruits."

"What do you know of our master?" Martha snapped.

"I know that he's evil. And all evil is at war with good. And in a war, both sides need soldiers. Let me be one. I'm tired of being the shy, quiet girl that nobody takes any notice of. I want to be an evil fucking bitch, like Martha Hamleigh."

Silence descended, and Sophie ached to see what was happening. Tom reminded her they were still only half way around the pews, so they got moving again.

Mia sounded convincing, but perhaps her expression was less so. Based on the audio alone, the girl deserved a BAFTA—or a one-off BBC drama at the very least. The girl had done good, now all there was left to do was wait.

"I like her," said Martha. "She reminds me of me. Emily would like her too. She does so love to corrupt the young."

"Or drown them," said Jonathan. "It can go either way with her."

"So," said Martha. "Do we let this little ball of enthusiasm hitch a saddle? Or feed her to Master?"

Sophie's gut swirled. This was it. And they still hadn't made it around the pews.

Jonathan grumbled. "I say we kill her and not waste any more time."

Martha tutted. "You spoilsport. Okay, have it your way."

"Wait!" said Mia. "I want to prove my worth. I want to show you what an evil bitch I can be."

"How?" asked Jonathan, sounding increasingly weary of the conversation.

"By telling you that the rest of the survivors from the crash are all sneaking up on you behind the pews."

Sophie and Tom froze, staring at one another in disbelief.

Mia had just given them up.

Gwen leapt up furiously. "You bitch!" she screamed. "You stupid fucking bitch!"

The jig was up.

CHAPTER 16

Tom stood with his hands in the air, not knowing what else to do. Sophie grabbed Gwen back before the girl did anything rash. Martha studied them like bugs. Jonathan seemed impressed.

"Give up," said Tom. "We're not letting you leave this place."

Martha howled with laughter. "Ha! Quiet, worm!" She waved a hand, and Tom felt something burn his mouth. When he tried to talk again, he couldn't part his lips. Sophie was staring at him, and he felt the stitches tighten. He mumbled in pain.

Gwen still focused only on Mia. "How could you screw my brother? How could you betray me like this? I don't know you at all."

Mia shrugged. "Better to reign in Hell. I want out of this place, but I don't want to go back to my old life." She turned to Martha. "Let me come with you."

Martha nodded. "If Jonathan has no problem with it, I think your heart might just be black enough."

Jonathan exhaled, letting it be known that he no longer cared. "Yes, the waif can join us, but you'll be the one training her, Martha."

"What should we do with her do-gooding companions?"

"What do you think, you silly *bint*? Feed them to Master. He'll need his strength."

"Of course. We need his favour now more than ever. Can't let Emily get all the glory."

Jonathan gave her a warning look. "Careful! She's already likely to have your head for strutting around like a peacock pretending to be her."

"A simple jest! Life gets dull down here."

"Then let us end the dullness."

Tom sensed their talking was at an end. He leapt up onto the end of the pew and used it to launch himself into the air.

And in the air he stayed.

Suspended.

Tom could not cry out with his lips stitched shut, but now he couldn't even struggle. He budged his eyes enough to see the ground hovering beneath him, three feet below the soles of his mud-caked shoes.

Martha had her finger pointed at him. "Behave, worm! Master will be here to devour you soon, just as soon as we remove the last of the pathetic spell on this place."

Tom peered off to the side and saw Sophie and Gwen circle round behind the altar. Jonathan spotted them and waved a hand casually, summoning forth a swarm of ants that engulfed Gwen and sent her into a panic, scratching at herself and screeching. Sophie avoided the insects, though, and launched an attack of her own. Both Martha and Jonathan turned on her, both with their hands held ready to weave magic.

Mia moved at the edge of Tom's vision, unseen by the others. Only he, in his elevated position, could see what she was doing. She was moving towards the altar.

Martha threw out her arms and sent a blast of hot air at Sophie. Sophie dodged up the steps beside the altar. Apparently magic took effort because Martha did not launch an immediate follow up attack. Instead, Jonathan stepped in to have his turn, lifting a fist above his head and beginning to chant loudly.

Mia grabbed a long, bone candle stick from the altar and brought it down on the back of Jonathan's skull before he finished his incantation. The crack rebounded around the cavernous church and made Tom wish he could wince. It was a hell of a hit.

Martha saw Mia's betrayal and yelled like a petulant child. She threw her hands up, ready to unleash another blast of magic, but Sophie was still coming for her, and the two woman—one an accountant, the other a witch—went tumbling against the altar, knocking it right over. Made of thick, heavy stone, it broke into two neat pieces and came to rest against the steps.

Tom dropped to the ground. He twisted both ankles and moaned as the stitches on his mouth vanished.

The church rumbled like a bomb blast had gone off nearby. Martha got on top of Sophie and raised a hand. Her nails grew three inches and glinted with sharpness—deadly daggers about to slice open fresh meat.

Mia swung the bone candle stick again and hit Martha square in the face. The witch went down but wasn't yet out. Even from on her back, she was still dangerous, and she spat a wad of saliva that turned to fire in mid-air. The glob hit Mia's hair and ignited it in a second, and soon her entire head was aflame. She screamed and cartwheeled, trying to put out the fire, but it was Gwen who came to her rescue. Her friend threw her to the ground and sprawled on top of her, suffocating the flames until they gave up the fight.

Mia had dropped the candle stick, but Sophie retrieved it. She swung it like a golf club and took the top of Martha's head clean off. The witch's skull crumpled like a ping pong ball.

Jonathan bellowed. "Martha! No, my dear Martha!" Sophie had to dodge out of the way as the warlock threw himself over the witch's body before turning his anger on her. "You worthless whore! Do you even understand the power and glory you have extinguished? Martha was worth a hundred of you. A thousand!"

Sophie glared right back at him. "You must be really devastated she's dead then."

Jonathan turned feral and launched himself at her. Tom threw himself along the ground and grabbed the warlock's ankle just in time to pull him back. Spitting fury, Jonathan turned sideways and booted Tom in the face with his other foot. His nose was already broken, but now it shattered. Sophie tried to hit Jonathan with the candle stick, but he turned in time to see it coming, and the weapon turned to dust in her hands.

The church kept rumbling, and a massive earthquake began. It shook Jonathan out of his fury and altered his mood to one of exultation. He looked up at the roof of the church and threw out his arms, speaking in tongues as if he had just discovered salvation.

"He is here. Chordaxis has escaped his prison."

The ceiling rained down on the nave, bone pieces and bits of stone falling all around them. The church was collapsing piece by piece, and they were trapped inside.

Mia got to her feet with Gwen's help. Her hair had burnt away to the scalp, but she had escaped any serious injury. Gwen held her, burying her grudge as quickly as she had forged it. Mia had been play acting the whole time, just like she said she would be. She'd been so good it had fooled them all.

But it hadn't been enough. Jonathan still lived, and Chordaxis was coming. The toad's ascent back to the world had not been prevented. Now what would happen?

Would the world burn?

Sophie dodged out of the way of a falling chunk of masonry just in time to avoid it killing her. "What's happening?" she said. "What is going on?"

Jonathan rose from the rubble. His grin was so wide it threatened to split his face. "The altar is broken. The totem housing the monk's spell is no more."

Tom grabbed the hysterical warlock and shook him. "What do you mean?"

"You fools! Just as Chordaxis focused his power through an altar, so did the monks focus their spell into one of their own. An altar is a vessel for mortals to commune with the gods. It is also a tether. Martha and I sought to diffuse the monk's spell carefully, but it seems brute force was just as good. Well done, worms, you have done my master's work for him."

Tom looked at the snapped altar and realised what they had done. Sophie looked distraught. Gwen and Mia held one another.

"Screw you," said Tom, winding up and punching Jonathan in the jaw. The warlock fell back into the rubble, laughing. The church continued to crumble around them.

Sophie grabbed his arm. "We have to leave."

He nodded, and he and the three women made a run for the wide aisle running through the centre of the nave. It rained brick and bone in front and behind them, and one of the pews reduced to smithereens when a massive roof beam flattened it. There was no way to know what would fall where, so all they could do was keep running—keep sprinting towards salvation, which was represented by a pair of thick wooden doors. Where did they lead?

Who cared?

"You cannot leave!" Jonathan shouted from behind them. Once again, he rose from the rubble, but his hysteria was at an end, and now he showed only unbridled fury on his face. He threw out both arms, and a torrent of ice flew over their heads. Tom grabbed Sophie, and the four of them ducked. The blast missed them and hit the thick wooden doors, freezing them instantly and encasing them in ice.

Their escape was ruined.

Jonathan stalked towards them, walking the aisle. Once again, his mask slipped, and a wretched, twisted face presented itself. His fingers were six inches long, and they fizzed and cracked with icy tendrils.

"Do you know when I first gave up on God?" he asked them. "When my sister died of cholera at the steps of the abbey. She was so sure the monks would save her, that God would see her goodness and reward her with life. But the doors to the monastery stayed closed. The abbot did not want disease under his roof. I struggled to reconcile myself with that for a long time. If God made man, then he also made disease—all part of his grand tapestry—so why would the abbot shy away from my dying sister? If it was God's will to sicken the monastery, then what was there to fear? Heaven awaits those who die holy, is that not the whole point?" He stopped walking. A chunk of concrete hit the ground right in front of him, cracking the floor.

Tom stepped forwards to face him. "Stop this, Jonathan. You don't have to give in to evil."

"I didn't give in to it, you fool. I begged for it. I saw the hypocrisy of the Church and turned away from an uncaring God. A better God found me one day beside the river. It was the day I tried to take my own life. Tying myself down with rocks and discarding my life was the biggest affront to God I could think of —but Chordaxis would not let me punish myself for another's sins. He took the water from the river and left it dry. Instead of drowning beneath the current, I found myself lying in the mud. Chordaxis spoke to me then. He told me that for every innocent soul I sent to him, he would grow in strength and reward me with strength of my own. He led me to others—my soulmates, Martha and Emily—and together we plotted damnation for the Church, and ascension for our beloved master. Chordaxis might serve his own agenda, but he is loyal to those who serve him. He does not abandon them or ignore them like your God does. He does not strike them down with cholera on the steps of a monastery."

Tom swallowed a lump in his throat. "I lost a sister too. I know how you feel."

"You know nothing!"

"Don't I? Her name was Zoe. She caught meningitis, a deadly disease just like cholera. God punished her for being an innocent child, one who tried to hide how sick she was feeling because she didn't want her birthday party cancelled." He shook his head bitterly. "She died the morning it was due, and it was cancelled anyway. She was eight. I was at university at the time. Never even got to say goodbye. Maybe if I'd been around, I would have seen how ill she was and got her to hospital faster. I'll never forgive my parents for being too busy to see what was wrong themselves. I'll never forgive myself either."

Jonathan's face quivered, the monster fading and his human face returning. His eyeballs quivered in his head as if they did not know where to look. "I am sorry for your loss."

Tom nodded. "And I for yours."

The warlock sighed. "There is an outlet for your grief, brother. Turn away from the black lies of your Lord, and join me in worshipping a fair and powerful master. He rises as we speak, and soon, the world will crumble before him. Only his servants shall remain free."

It was almost tempting to Tom. What life did he have to go back to, anyway? Sophie would start her new life as a divorcee, and he'd be left alone. Concentrating on work would seem frivolous after all he had witnessed, and even without the events following the car crash, it had still been pointless. What use was money and success if you had no one to share it with? No wife. And never any children.

But real power? If what Jonathan said was true, then what could the future be? Eternal life, perhaps? Extreme wealth and influence, or just plain old domination? He could have a hundred new wives and a legion of children if he only agreed to serve the same master Jonathan did. The way he saw it, there would only be one downside.

He would never be able to look in a mirror again.

Jonathan could sense Tom considering it because he locked eyes with him and nodded. "You can have whatever you wish for. There is only one thing you must do."

"What?"

Jonathan nodded at Sophie. "I will not let Martha's murder go unanswered. Take the whore's life, and you may all join me. Only one of you must die."

Tom turned to his wife and saw the worried look on her face. Did she expect him to do it? Maybe he could? Was it a sacrifice worth making?

Sophie swallowed and rubbed at her throat. "Tom?"

Tom shook his head. "I'm sorry. I'm sorry that I can't do as you ask, Jonathan."

Jonathan's face flickered, and his gruesome visage returned—his features twisted by evil once again. "A pity, but the offer is not yet fully declined."

Tom frowned. "What do you mean?"

"He means me," said Gwen. Through all the chaos she had kept a hold of the testicle loppers, and she now lifted them over her head. "He means I can kill Sophie and take the deal, even if you won't."

Tom tried to grab Gwen, but he was too taken by surprise. Sophie, too, was confused and reacted slowly. Gwen opened the blades and swung their long iron handle. The sharp instrument cut through the air with an audible hiss.

And then it was flying out of her hands.

Tom felt the air move as the metal blades whipped passed him and embedded themselves in Jonathan's neck. The warlock took several steps backwards, shocked dumb by the blood suddenly leaking out of him. His human face came back again, pale and afraid. Gwen strode forward until she was standing right in front of him. He tried to raise a hand, but there was no magic in his finger-tips, and she batted it away as if he were a child. She looked into his dark eyes and spoke.

"This is for Stacey, bitch!"

She grabbed the testicle remover by the handles and clamped them shut. The blades sliced through the rest of Jonathan's neck as if it were butter. His head slid backwards off his shoulders and landed in the rubble at his feet. His headless corpse flopped forwards and landed in the centre of the aisle. Blood spurted from the neck stump for a moment, then crystallised into ice. Gwen nudged Jonathan's head with her foot. It too was turning to ice.

Tom placed a hand on her back. "Good throw."

"Not really."

Tom frowned. "What do you mean?"

"I was aiming for his testicles."

Mia called out to get their attention. "Look!"

Tom turned. The wooden doors were unfrozen, Jonathan's magic dispelled. The church had stopped crumbling, and there was hardly a ceiling left. In fact, when Tom looked up, he saw the dreary grey sky. The one that had hung over him since waking up on the riverbed—the grey, featureless sky that would soon hang over the entire world if Chordaxis were allowed to escape.

"It's not over," he said.

And as if in agreement, the thick wooden doors blew inward and flew from their hinges. The debris of the church lifted off the ground and made it hard to see. Tom reached out blindly for Sophie and found her hand. He fell against her, his various wounds merging into one giant agony.

"Tom, don't leave my side, okay?"

He pulled her closer. "Never."

The dust settled, a cloud of it travelling out of the open doorway into the grey, featureless dusk. Slowly, a shape began to form outside the church.

CHAPTER 17

The cloud of dust settled back on the ruined floor of the church, and Sophie could finally see again. She peered out of the ruined doorway and watched someone approach.

Emily Tanner was bathed in flames—the spirit of fire turned flesh. She marched towards the church with single purpose, passing through the stone cavern outside that seemed to stretch on forever. Overhead, the image of a bridge fizzled in and out. Black shapes moved along it back and forth. The barrier between this place and the other was breaking down. Whatever held this hell together was crumbling along with the church.

"It's Emily," said Gwen.

Sophie nodded. "She's here to take her reward. Father Cotton is dead, and his church is in ruins. There's nothing to stop Chordaxis rising back to earth now."

Gwen sneered. "With Jonathan and Martha gone, she'll get all the credit."

Emily climbed the steps before the church. The stench of burning flesh made Sophie gag. It was the same rotten stench she'd first smelt outside the house beneath the bridge. Emily had been near then too, but trapped inside the tree. Instead, they had encountered a woman using her name, Martha Hamleigh. The authentic Emily Tanner was far worse than the mockery. Her flesh burnt and flaked off in the wind, filling the air with buzzing embers. Black coals stood in for her eyes, and they swirled with hatred. Hatred for all things.

"She looks madder than last time we saw her," said Mia, reaching for her hair but then seeming to remember it was gone.

"Yeah," said Tom, standing right at Sophie's side. "I suppose she doesn't like it when we kill her friends."

Gwen clenched her fists. "Well we don't like it when she kills ours either."

"Emily, stop!" Sophie shouted. "You can't leave this place. People will die if you don't keep this place together. I know you have the power. You can make this right again."

Emily gave no impression she had heard.

"Stop!" Sophie repeated. "I understand why you became what you are. You were a woman living in a time when being a woman was little more than being a dog. I can't imagine what it was like. You must have felt powerless, so no wonder you sought strength wherever you could. But Chordaxis is a monster, and innocent people will die if he returns to the world. And that world isn't the one you know. Women are free and beautiful now. We can do whatever we want with our lives. Men do not own us, and we are no longer obligated to pop out children and look after a man. That's what put the anger inside you, right? I see no other reason a powerful woman like you would make themselves a slave to a self-serving toad."

Emily stopped. The flames surrounding her petered out and she was suddenly a small woman looking at them. "You understand nothing of my anger, but know that it was legendary in my time and shall be again in yours. All will tremble at the name Emily Tanner."

Sophie shook her head. She pitied the woman. "No, they won't. People don't care about witches and gods and magic anymore. We have television, and KFC, and fucking tanks!"

Emily frowned.

"Exactly," said Sophie. "You don't even know what you'll be walking into. The world is more terrifying now than you could ever imagine. Cell phones, the Internet, self-driving cars... It's Hell. Far more than this place is."

"You speak in riddles, wench! The world will become what I make it."

"You mean what your master makes it. You are not in charge of your own destiny. What makes you different from any other love-struck girl?"

Emily hissed, and flames reignited on her flesh. "Do not mistake my faith for childish emotions. I know whom I serve, and he is glorious. I will reign by Chordaxis's side—his infernal bride."

"Fuck that," said Mia. "Why should you have to marry a toad just to share some power he lets you have?"

"Silence!" Emily threw out her arms and twin blasts of fire leapt out. Mia, Gwen, Tom, and Sophie all spilled in separate directions.

Sophie scrambled behind a large chunk of bone that had fallen from the church wall. "Guess they didn't have feminism in her day," she shouted to the others. "That's okay, we can still teach her about girl power."

Gwen threw a rock that struck Emily in the shoulder. "Yeah, take that, bitch!"

Tom scrambled over to Sophie, dodging another blast of fire. "Got any more fire extinguishers?"

"Not unless you have a magic altar on you."

Tom looked back down the ruined nave, now a pile of rubble. "Sorry, you broke the last one."

She shrugged. "You crashed the car. We're even."

"About that," he said, looking pained. "During the crash, you were—"

Another blast of fire hit close and sent a storm of stone chips and bone their way. Sophie scrambled behind more cover. "Now's not a time for talking, Tom!"

"You shall be my toys," said Emily. "I shall drag you behind me on chains like poor Father Cotton dragged the woman and children of Abbeydale."

"It's called Cottontree now," Sophie shouted. "They must have named it after him, but looks like they forgot all about you."

"Ha! Because I never revealed myself. I wore the face of an

innocent woman until the end. This time shall be different. This time I shall display myself as Queen."

"We already have a queen, and she'd wipe the floor with you!"

Tom frowned at her, hiding a few feet away behind a fallen pew. "You hate the Royal Family."

Sophie scowled at him. "I'd muck out their stables if it means getting out of here."

The ground rocked beneath their feet, tilting to and fro. It felt like they were being lifted.

"Chordaxis comes," cried Emily. "Your time is at an end. God is trembling."

"You worship a fucking frog," said Gwen, peering out from the rubble. "Do you know how much of a loser that makes you?"

Emily stood in the centre aisle, distracted by Gwen's insult. Sophie grabbed a chunk of rock and threw it at Emily. It missed and hit the ground at her feet. Emily threw an arm in her direction and blasted fire. A half-toppled pillar blackened in the heat.

Gwen popped up and threw another rock. It hit Emily on the back of the head. The girl had lethal aim. The witch barked and spun back around. This time she didn't throw up her arms. She just yelled in fury. "I shall eviscerate you!"

Sophie dodged behind the overturned pew where Tom was hiding. She told him what she was thinking. "She has to recharge."

He shook his head at her. "What?"

"Every time Emily uses magic, she takes ten seconds to recharge. She can't keep blasting away."

"Great! So, she can only try to cook us six times a minute."

"It means," said Sophie, "that she's only dangerous ten percent of the time."

Tom saw her point. "Okay, good. So how do we use that?"

"We keep pissing her off!"

Mia cried out somewhere in the church. Sophie peered around the pew and realised Emily had found the girl's hiding place and had sent a swarm upon her. A cloud of embers buzzed around her, singeing her flesh and summoning angry welts all over her face.

"It burns!" she cried. "Help me."

Sophie broke cover. Tom tried to stop her, but she knew her attack had to be now. Emily had just used her powers, and that left a window while she regathered her powers. She barged the witch right in the centre of her back. Emily was totally unprepared by the blindside attack, and her small body went crashing into the rubble. She hit her head on a wedge of broken bone and blood exploded from her forehead. The blow stunned her, and she didn't even swear or cry out. Sophie lifted her foot, ready to stamp the bitch's lights out.

There was a blinding flash and Sophie's foot came down on hard stone. Her heel crunched, but the pain didn't matter. Emily was gone.

"You think you can defy me, foolish woman!"

Sophie turned. Emily stood right beside her, blood cascading from the ragged, sucking wound on her forehead. She might have been small, but Emily Tanner could pack a punch and the blow struck Sophie between her breasts and knocked the wind out of her. She slumped into the rubble, heaving and gasping.

Tom launched himself at Emily, striking her across the face. It felt strange seeing him hit a woman, for it was something she would never have dreamt of him doing, but now she egged him on, hoping he found chance to hit her again. Emily reeled, but Tom wasn't quick enough to follow up. She threw out an arm and let out another blast of fire.

The noise Tom made was sickening. He fell onto his knees, clutching his face. Sophie still hadn't caught her breath, but she clambered over to him now.

When she saw the blistered flesh on his face she yelped. "Tom!"

The ground shook again.

Emily stood over them, hands raised. "You have no idea what this place is, do you?"

The sight of Tom's ruined face had taken the fight out of Sophie. "Just end this nightmare already."

Emily sneered. "The nightmares are only just beginning."

"Eat shit and die," said Gwen, emerging from the rubble behind Emily.

Sophie flinched as blood spattered her face.

Something appeared out of Emily's chest suddenly. The witch glanced down at herself curiously, even raising a befuddled eyebrow.

"This will not do!" she uttered and then fell sideways into the rubble. She was still alive, but babbling in shock. The fight was over.

Sophie turned her attention back to Tom, who was moaning with pain. "Tom! Tom, can you look at me?"

His hands were shaking, but he moved them away from his face. His right eye was milky, the eyelids below and above a sickly shade of pink. The left eye blinked, iris and pupil still intact. "I can't see you very well," he said. "It's blurry."

She caressed his arm. "Close your right eye, honey."

He did as she told him. "It's not blurry anymore."

His face was a mess, and his right eye was ruined, but at least he wasn't blind. Sophie pulled him into a hug for the benefit of her own relief than for his comfort. "We did it. We beat them."

"Um, guys. I don't think we did?" Gwen was standing near the opening where the wooden doors had blown in. She stared out at the featureless cavern outside the church. There was movement out there.

Sophie climbed to her feet, stepping around Emily who was still clutching onto life. She left Tom sitting, not wanting to test his balance or strength after losing an eye. She went over to join Gwen on her own. Mia watched from a few feet away, her hands fiddling as if she wanted something to hold.

"Chordaxis is coming," said Sophie.

The ground outside shifted, and something was coming up. This was not the creature they had encountered in the cellar, but something far bigger. Its one arm alone, clawing its way up out of the ground, was the size of a bus. The back of its head rose from the stone like a wrecking ball.

"It's the size of Godzilla," said Gwen. "How do we fight something like that?"

Sophie couldn't take her eyes off the massive beast rising from its grave. No living thing on earth possessed such size, and she doubted if even a squadron of tanks could put a dent in it. And she was responsible for it being released. Emily would never have been liberated from the Hickory Tree and Father Cotton would not be dead if not for her and Tom.

"What have we done?"

"Hey, I didn't do anything," said Gwen. "And neither did you. The shit that caused all this went down hundreds of years ago, and we got dragged in the middle of it."

The creature continued to rise, revealing itself as larger than any of them could ever have imagined. It truly was a god. Sophie wanted to move, but all she could do was feebly ask questions. "How is this possible? How did we end up here? How do we stop it?"

"We pray," said Mia, stumbling through the rubble. Her face was a bright red tapestry of singed skin, but her eyes were wide open, clear and determined.

"What do you mean?" asked Gwen.

Mia stopped beside a long pew broken in two and leant on it for support. "Chordaxis has been trapped here for hundreds of years because the monks prayed to God to help them. Why can't we do the same?"

"Because we're not monks," said Sophie.

"So? Is a prayer not a prayer? The monks weren't magic. They just prayed together, and God listened. Why wouldn't he listen now?"

"Well," said Sophie. "For one thing, I'm an atheist. I don't think God listens to people who don't believe in him."

Mia smiled grotesquely, her lips swollen and red. "Really? Outside that door is a real-life god—a demon maybe, but certainly not human. We are standing in a broken-down church in Hell. You seriously don't believe in God after all that? Is this not proof?"

Sophie opened her mouth to speak. The thought of acknowledging God made her cringe. It was so stupid to believe in a religion that in her eyes was nothing more than organised panhandling. Yet... "I suppose I do believe. How can I not? But that still doesn't change the fact I have never believed in him before."

Gwen shrugged her shoulders. "I never believed either, but isn't that the whole thing with God? If you come to his embrace, then all is forgiven? Doesn't matter what we did or did not believe before."

Sophie could look out at the massive beast no longer. She turned away and closed her eyes, trying to squeeze the sight from her mind. When she opened them again, everyone was looking at her, as if she somehow had the deciding vote on what to do next.

She shrugged her shoulders. "Okay, we pray. What else is left?"

⚜

THEY HURRIED DOWN THE AISLE, DODGING THROUGH THE rubble. All of them sported wounds, but it was Tom who suffered most. His right hand was pierced through and infected. His right eye was ruined. And the centre of his face was dominated by a broken nose. The worst of Sophie's injuries was an increasing pain in her throat. It had started with a tickle when this whole thing had started, but now it was constant agony.

"The altar must be buried under all this rubble," said Gwen, kicking aside the smaller chunks of bone and stone. They started digging, working together to move the larger debris. The entire time, the sound of the earth moving outside continued. The remaining chunks of wall and ceiling fell down, and Sophie cried out when a wedge of stone struck her shoulder. It left her arm limp and burning—a dislocation probably, but it didn't stop her digging, and she continued one-handed. Soon the walls of the church stood only four-feet high, and the ceiling had all fallen, exposing the sky where it poked through the top of the cavern. How they had survived the building's implosion was hard to fathom. Perhaps God really was looking out for them.

"It's here," said Tom, shoving aside the last layer of debris and uncovering one half of the stone altar. Moments later, Mia chirped that she had found the other half. They tried to lift the pieces together, but the thing was too heavy. Behind them, Chordaxis began to roar. The beast was free.

"Leave it in two pieces," said Sophie. "We'll just have to hope for the best. Let's pray. Who's going to start?"

Gwen stared at her. "What?"

"Pray!"

"How? I never did before."

Sophie's jaw dropped as she realised she had no idea how to pray either. Surely it was more than just closing her eyes and speaking to God?

"I'll lead us," said Mia. "Close your eyes everyone."

Sophie was almost too afraid to oblige. Chordaxis's roars grew louder, and the ground shook rhythmically behind them as if some great beast stomped the earth. With her eyes closed, she had no idea how close her death was.

Mia began. "In the name of Allah, the Gracious, the Merciful. When the sun is wrapped up, and when the stars are obscured, and when the mountains are made to move, and when the she-camels, tenmonth pregnant, are abandoned, and when the beasts are gathered together, and when the seas are made to flow forth one into the other, and when people are brought together, and when the heaven is laid bare, and when the Fire is caused to blaze up—"

"It's not working," said Gwen.

The beast's roars got closer. Sophie felt its breath gusting down the aisle. Felt it's footsteps rattle the earth. But she kept her eyes shut—nothing she wanted to see now. Let he death be sudden and unexpected.

Mia ignored the interruption and carried on, but it no longer sounded like she was reciting. "Allah—God—Lord Almighty, we are four souls undeserving of your love, yet we beg for it. We are undeserving of your protection, yet we plead for it. We are undeserving of your gift, yet we cling to it. Provide us shelter so we may live in worship of you, and fight back the darkness so we may see."

Rocks hit Sophie, tossed up from the aisle. The ground shook like a drumbeat as giant footsteps picked up speed and raced towards them. Chordaxis roared loud enough to blot out all other sound from the world, and Sophie could no longer hear Mia's words. So she shouted some of her own. "Save us, Father. Please!"

The roaring stopped.

The ground stopped shaking.

Sophie kept her eyes shut, too terrified to risk seeing something she would never forget. She felt as though she were sitting in the eye of a storm—a momentary calm before her life got wrenched away from her. She cried out when something touched her arm, and it wasn't until she heard Tom's voice that she realised it was just his hand on her elbow.

"It's okay, Soph. You can open your eyes."

Even with the assurance of her husband, she still didn't want to see, but eventually she could bear the darkness no more.

They were still in the church. But the church had been rebuilt. Gone were the bone-carved pews and grizzly features. Gone was the harsh stone. Now, the church resembled St. Martins where she had been baptised as a child. In fact, she was pretty sure it was the same building. The layout matched exactly—it was merely older, with no modern lights or tapestries on the wall. It was a church from the time when churches were being built.

Father Cotton stood at the back of the church, up on the raised section behind the altar. The altar itself was fixed, upright once again. The priest looked at peace, his hands clasped in front of him as he approached. "You did the Lord's work, and for that, He is pleased."

Sophie reached out to grab something, but there was nothing nearby, so she toppled onto her hands. The four of them looked up at the priest from on their knees, too tired to stand.

"You're alive," said Tom.

Father Cotton shook his head. "Not at all, but I am here no less. My church is restored, and there is no place I would rather be. Emily Tanner's curse upon Abbeydale is lifted. My flock has finally passed on. Thank you."

"Then why are you still here?" Gwen asked.

"To watch over this place. Chordaxis still dwells in this place and will continue to. I am to be his keeper. My humanity restored, I am shod of my monstrous affliction, and may move about this place freely. I would see you safely gone from here."

"What is this place?" asked Sophie.

Father Cotton smiled. "It is what you always believed it to be. It is Hell. But not yours. Your place is not here. So, leave."

At the other end of the church, thick wooden doors opened, and sunlight shone in from outside. Sophie made another attempt to get up, and this time she made it to her feet. She studied the priest suspiciously. "We can really leave?"

He nodded, then waved a hand towards the doors.

Gwen, Mia, Tom, and Sophie linked up, arms around one another, and started up the aisle. Their progress was slow, their bodies failing them with every step, but they pushed on together, keeping each other upright. With each passing second, Sophie expected the church to fall back down on them, but the closer she got to that glorious sunlight coming through the doors, the more she dared to hope.

Could the nightmare finally be over?

She held on to Tom and didn't let go.

CHAPTER 18

Tom stepped through the doors into the light and looked up at the sun. It was the sun that told him it was over. There were no tricks, curses, or spells—sunlight had returned to this place and pushed back the darkness.

They found themselves back on the riverbed, but the mud was no longer black and sucking, but firm and brown. The bridge spanned overhead, just twenty feet above. The black shapes flitted back and forth, but it was now clear they were people—faces gawping over the edge. Responders to the car crash perhaps?

People who came to help us, thought Tom.

"The banks are only twelve feet high," said Gwen. "We can climb out."

Father Cotton appeared in the doorway of the church, his hands hidden inside the wide cuffs of his habit. "Yes, my children, you may. This place captured you in your trauma and took you out of the natural order. Climb the banks and return to your rightful places."

Mia turned back to face him. "We'll go back to the car crash? What if we're hurt?"

Father Cotton smiled, but gave no other expression. "Your fates are unknown to me, but they are yours to claim."

Sophie shrugged. "Better than staying here, whatever happens."

Tom thought that was a little insensitive to Father Cotton, the new custodian of this place, but he was inclined to agree. Life was calling, and he wanted to run to it.

In the distance, he saw the house. It was no longer beneath the bridge, and the blackened oak tree was gone. It had no windows or doors—a prison now.

"Shall we go together?" Sophie asked him.

He nodded. "Back to our old lives. Still want me to drop you off at your sisters?"

She smiled. "Of course not. Our marriage has been through Hell, but we're about to step back into the light."

Tom leant over and kissed her. He had loved her for half a lifetime, longer than he could remember. His life had changed the day he had met her, and all that came before was a misty haze to him now. It was because of how long he had loved her that he knew in his heart that she didn't love him back—not anymore. She would call off the divorce, he believed in that, but she would do so out of loyalty and obligation formed of this place that had forced them to unwillingly depend on each other. She'd grow old and miserable with him, instead of embarking on the new life she yearned for.

It was time to let her go.

But not just yet. He reached out and took her hand.

Gwen and Mia hurried up the embankment, the youngest and least weary of the group. Tom was happy to watch them go, and he wondered if they would all remember each other once they woke up back where they were supposed to be. Would their memories of the house beneath the bridge wipe clean, or would they recall every moment? It was hard to say which he would prefer.

Sophie nudged him. "Tom, look!"

Tom smiled. As Mia neared the top of the embankment, her burnt hair regrew, and her injured skin healed. She walked into a delicate shaft of light and faded away slowly. A step behind her, Gwen's mud-stained clothes washed themselves back to their original colours, and then she began to fade away too. Within a couple of seconds, both girls were gone.

Sophie smiled at Tom, squeezed his hand. "Our turn."

He nodded, and they took the final steps up the embankment. Near the top, his chest tingled. Sophie coughed and rubbed at her neck. A light shone over him, and he had to squint against its intensity. He glanced at Sophie because he wanted to pass through with her at the exact same moment, but he noticed the same light did not shine on her. A thin red line appeared across her throat.

Then leaked blood.

Sophie's eyes went wide. She gripped her throat and started choking.

Tom froze, going no further into the light. What was happening? He glanced back at the church and saw Father Cotton watching them sadly. Then he looked the other way and saw...

The car crash.

All three vehicles had crashed into the river, but the water was too low to submerge them. Tom saw himself moaning in the driver's seat. He saw Patrick and Brandon, too, in their truck. Patrick was sprawled over the steering wheel and clutching his chest—looked like he was having a heart attack.

Was that why the builder had been so out of breath?

Brandon was crushed beneath the bodywork where the truck had crumpled against the bridge before flipping over into the river. The third car involved in the accident was small and pink, and full of girls. He was surprised to see Gwen and Mia getting out into the knee-high water. They were relatively unhurt, and they stared into the wreckage at their friend Stacey, whose face had sliced away from her skull in an impact with the side window. She was dead.

Then there was Sophie. Sitting beside him, her head had been sliced nearly clean off by the shovel.

No. No, she can't be dead. She can't be gone.

Tom grabbed Sophie beside him at the top of the river bank and shoved her backwards. She cried out in surprise and went tumbling down the hill. It was a bad fall, and she ended up at the bottom in a half-conscious heap. He ran down the hill after her, but not to help her. He went and grabbed Father Cotton.

"What the fuck is this?"

"It is not my doing," said the priest calmly, even as he was shaken fiercely. "You should not be here. You should be there."

Tom shook the man harder, making his bald head rock back and forth. "Sophie is dead back there."

"Then dead she must be."

"No! When I tried to leave here, there was a light. It was only on me."

"Light is for the living."

Tom looked back at Sophie, winded and clutching herself on the floor. With tears in his eyes, he turned back to the priest and tried to understand what tricks were being played. But he saw nothing but truth and compassion in the man's eyes. "No! Please, no. Let her come back with me."

"It is not within my power, child. I wish it were."

Tom fought back sobs. "W-what? What will happen to her?"

"She must remain here. Her afterlife started the moment you all woke up here."

"She deserves Heaven."

"Nobody deserves Heaven. It must be earned. And she has not earned it. If she were alive, she could leave this place, but the dead must remain where they find themselves. But fret not, the evil is gone from this place, and I shall give her companionship. It is more than some get."

"No. This is Hell. She can't stay here with only you as company."

"It is not Hell any longer," said Father Cotton. "It is merely a place. That is all. Go, child. Your time is not yet at an end. This is her fate, not yours. I felt the sadness in you as you left. She does not love you anymore. You know it in your heart."

Tom swallowed more grief than he had ever felt in his life. "No, she doesn't love me. But I love her. I refuse the light."

Father Cotton seemed shocked. "Be careful of what you ask. If you do not leave now, you shall never leave. This will be your eternity."

Tom looked back at Sophie and remembered the young girl who had cleaned vomit off him before listening to his problems until three in the morning. The woman who had tried so hard to give him a family and a life but had received nothing in return. He turned back to Father Cotton and did not blink. "I refuse the light. I choose her."

Father Cotton nodded his head and turned away. "My church is open to you both. May God bless you."

"He already has."

Tom hurried over to Sophie's side. She was still hurt, and he expected her to fly at him when he got to her, but she seemed only confused. "T-Tom? What happened? I... felt funny. My throat hurt."

Tom looked at her. The red line had gone. So had the bridge and the dark shapes moving along it. His opportunity to leave had expired, but he did not care. Where the bridge had stood, something else had taken its place. There was a house, and he knew it was meant for them. It was a cosy little cottage with a hot tub outside and a swinging bench hanging from two vibrant apple trees. The sun beat down and cast a healing warmth.

It was the type of place he and Sophie had once dreamt of retiring to, but the truth was he'd never expected to actually end up there. Looked like retirement had come to him instead. Somehow, he knew Father Cotton had provided the house as a gift. It was perfect. Maybe Hell wouldn't be so bad after all.

He wrapped his arms around Sophie and held her tight, kissing the top of her head. "Everything's okay," he said. "We have each other, and that's all that matters."

"I love you, Tom."

He winced. "I love you too, Soph. I love you too."

<<<>>>

WANT FREE BOOKS?

Don't miss out on your FREE Iain Rob Wright horror starter pack. Five free bestselling horror novels sent straight to your inbox. No strings attached.

For more information just visit this page:
www.iainrobwright.com/free-starter-pack/

In addition, you can also save money by purchasing my books in extra-value box sets. Grab yours now.

Boxset 1
Sam, ASBO, The Final Winter, The Housemates, Sea Sick

Boxset 2
Ravage, Savage, Animal Kingdom, The Picture Frame, 2389, The Peeling Omnibus, Slasher, Soft Target, A-Z of Horror Vol 1

PLEA FROM THE AUTHOR

Hey, Reader. So you got to the end of my book. I hope that means you enjoyed it. Whether or not you did, I would just like to thank you for giving me your valuable time to try and entertain you. I am truly blessed to have such a fulfilling job, but I only have that job because of people like you; people kind enough to give my books a chance and spend their hard-earned money buying them. For that I am eternally grateful.

If you would like to find out more about my other books then please visit my website for full details. You can find it at:

www.iainrobwright.com.

Also feel free to contact me on Facebook, Twitter, or email (all details on the website), as I would love to hear from you.

If you enjoyed this book and would like to help, then you could think about leaving a review on Amazon, Goodreads, or anywhere else that readers visit. The most important part of how well a book sells is how many positive reviews it has, so if you leave me one then you are directly helping me to continue on this journey as a fulltime writer. Thanks in advance to anyone who does. It means a lot.

Iain Rob Wright is one of the UK's most successful horror and suspense writers, with novels including the critically acclaimed, THE FINAL WINTER; the disturbing bestseller, ASBO; and the wicked screamfest, THE HOUSEMATES.

His work is currently being adapted for graphic novels, audio books, and foreign audiences. He is an active member of the Horror Writer Association and a massive animal lover.

www.iainrobwright.com
FEAR ON EVERY PAGE

For more information
www.iainrobwright.com
iain.robert.wright@hotmail.co.uk

Printed in Great Britain
by Amazon